A YOUNG LADY
SHOULD BE OBEDIENT

said Phoebe's parents, as they sent her off to the vast estate of the infamous Duke of Grade, where he was free to do with her what he would

A YOUNG LADY
SHOULD BE GRATEFUL

said the Duke as he dangled his huge fortune as a reward for Phoebe's following his every whim and catering to his every desire

A YOUNG LADY
SHOULD BE ROMANTIC

said the notorious London rake and military hero Captain Brent Maitland, as he covered Phoebe's lips with his in a passionate kiss, and ravenously awaited the result

A YOUNG LADY
SHOULD BE EVERYTHING
THAT PHOEBE WAS NOT

as she turned the Duke from master into servant, informed the Captain that he was free to seek his pleasure elsewhere—and silently prayed that her triumphs would not cause her to lose all that she hungered for . . .

The Poor Relation

Margaret SeBastian

POPULAR LIBRARY • NEW YORK

Published by Popular Library, a unit of CBS Publications, the Consumer Publishing Division of CBS Inc.

May, 1978

ISBN: 0-445-04222-2

Chapter I

"MR. GRANTHAM, what ever are we going to do now?" pleaded Mrs. Grantham, casting a beseeching look towards her husband across the breakfast table.

Mr. Grantham poked his head from behind the journal he was holding up before him and stared vacantly at his better half.

"Eh what, m' dear? You were saying?" he inquired.

"Well, I wish you would advise me as to what we are going to do about it now?"

"What now? Do what now? Really, Lydia, I have not the vaguest notion of what anything now! I should take it as a kindness if you would let me finish with the newspaper so that I can go through this morning's post."

"I do declare, Mr. Grantham, you are positively heartless. You know full well what I have reference to! Yet you sit there, that London sheet ever so much more important to you, while the world about you is in a fair way to collapse! Oh, heartless father, indeed!"

Phoebe, their only child, a young lady of seventeen springs, sat looking at her mother. Her head was cocked slightly, and her expression puzzled. She turned her attention to her father to hear his response.

Mr. Grantham very carefully put down his paper

and donned a look of infinite patience as he removed his spectacles from the bridge of his nose.

"I have a strange feeling that you are not about to do me the kindness I requested—and heaven only knows when and if I shall get to the post—My dear," he expostulated, lifting up the small collection of unopened letters laying at the side of his plate, "I must get to the post. I am sure that whatever this dire event is which is about to overwhelm our household, it will be neither augmented nor diminished one iota if you were to postpone this interruption of my matutinal habits for an hour, say."

"Heartless! You are thoroughly heartless! To be able to sit and ponder the fate of that madman, when you know perfectly well our most noble Duke of Wellington has already seen to him, has got to be a piece of the greatest idiocy I have ever heard of! Leave that wild Frenchman to his Grace and cast your eyes upon this sweet child before you, your own precious daughter! Wellington will look after Monsieur Bonaparte, but who, I ask you, is going to look after our darling daughter after I am gone?"

A certain air of trial came into Mr. Grantham's countenance as he smiled a tight little smile and responded: "Well, my dear, I shall certainly do my very best by her, I assure you—but I expect it is not a contingency we need concern ourselves with particularly for some time yet."

"What has that to say to anything when it is upon us now, this very minute—"

"What in blazes are you getting at, Lydia?" he demanded as he began to lose patience.

Mrs. Grantham was undaunted. She pointed her finger at him. "Will you listen to the man? It was but yesterday we attended the services for dear, dear

Aunt Harewood, and he sits there in all peace and tranquility and never lifts a finger nor is he about to!"

"I assure you, Mrs. Grantham, this is not my idea of peace and tranquility, and no, I am not about to lift my finger for I still have not the least notion what great calamity is about to descend upon us!"

"Mama, what has happened?" asked Phoebe, very curious but not upset in the least.

"Hush, child, I am talking to your father, your very heartless father."

"Dearest Lydia, heart of my life, I pray you will inform me what Lady Harewood's obsequies have got to do with us beyond the fact that the old girl was one of your high-blooded relations."

"Oh, Jonathan, how can you be so dense!"

"Not because I try, m' love. Why don't you tell me what is on your mind and at least give me a fair chance to try to understand this awful thing. After all, Lady Harewood was in her seventies, I am sure, and while I am duly sorry to see her go, at her advanced age, it is not unusual, even for a Harewood. We all of us have to go sometime, and I suspect, considering that horror of a life she must have led with that miserable excuse, your precious Uncle Janus, she truly has been laid to a well-earned rest."

"But that is just the point, you silly man! Aunt Sophia was housekeeper to Uncle Janus for as long as anyone can remember. What is the poor man going to do by himself, alone in that great big house?"

"Lydia, I absolutely forbid it! Don't you dare to entertain the idea for one minute of him coming to live with us! I cannot stand the fellow, even making allowance for his exalted rank!"

Mrs. Grantham gave vent to a burst of superior laughter. "How utterly ridiculous of you to ever think

7

it! The Duke of Grade to come live with us? I should live to see the day!"

"Well, I hope *I* shall not!"

Phoebe giggled.

Mr. Grantham chuckled in satisfaction at her approval of his wit.

Mrs. Grantham glared at them both.

"Oh, so you think it is all a lark, young lady, do you?" she charged. "Well, I bid you think on this: Your father is not made of money, and it was ever our hope that Uncle Janus would see to it that you were provided with a proper marriage portion. Now do you understand my concern, *Mistress* Grantham? Now do you see all that there is to laugh at and make jests with your thoughtless father?"

Phoebe shook her head in puzzlement. "No, Mama, truly I do not see what any of this has to do with poor Aunt Harewood's passing."

"Then truly are you your father's daughter, for, from the look of him, I venture to say he has not an inkling of a clue to what I am talking about."

"My dear, that is the first thing you have said that makes any sense to me, and I agree with you wholeheartedly. Precisely what does Lady Harewood's passing have to do with my daughter's dowry?"

Mrs. Grantham sighed gustily and began to explain the facts of the world to her nearest and dearest.

"Aunt Sophia was Uncle Janus's housekeeper. Now he does not have one. At his age, he certainly must procure a female to take Aunt Sophia's place, and, as she will not be his sister, no matter under what pretense she comes to him, she is bound to remain his wife. Now do you see?"

Mr. Grantham was suddenly quite sober. He screwed up his mouth and nodded. "Quite."

Phoebe shook her head vigorously. "But I do not see a thing, Mama. Where is the connection?"

"Oh, precious," mourned Mrs. Grantham, "you have so much to learn! Can you believe for one minute that some strange woman, newly elevated to the rank and title of Duchess of Grade, will have any thought for the welfare of the Harewoods once she is dowager?"

"What is that to us, Mama? You are a Harewood, surely you must gain some share in his Grace's property—"

"Oh, heavens, no, my dear! What is entailed to the Harewoods goes to your great-uncle's nearest male kin—" she paused and plunged into thought "—now let me see! Why, he would be your cousin twice removed, I do believe. Is that not so, Jonathan?"

"Young Maitland? I imagine so," he replied, "but he is your relation, not mine!"

"At any rate, it is a quite distant branch of the Harewoods that is in the direct line, so, you see, it cannot do *us* the least bit of good for some strange female to make her appearance at this stage. Whatever shall we do?"

Said Phoebe: "I do not care. His Grace is a grouchy old thing, and I should be just as pleased not to be beholden to him for anything!"

"How very noble of you to say so!" exclaimed Mrs. Grantham irritably. "As if you even know what you are saying! You do have a wish to be married, Miss, do you not?"

"I am sure when the time comes for me to wed, I shall not have the least trouble—"

"La! Will you not? And who, pray, will marry you if you are but a penniless gentlewoman?"

"Mama, I have no manner of use for gentlemen who

9

are only concerned with riches and gain. My gentleman will offer for me just as I am," retorted Phoebe.

"Bah! You babble like a babe, my dear! Love will never provide sustenance for your children, and I know whereof I speak! Just look at *us*! Your father and I are in no position to afford more than a paltry thousand to see you wed. We were sure that Uncle Janus was going to do well by you! Oh, whatever shall we do? I do not think I could bear to see my only jewel the bride of some gentleman of no rank and less means."

"Oh, but Mama—" Phoebe began to protest when her father interrupted.

"No, my child, your mother is right. The consequences of his Grace finding himself another housekeeper is bound to have devastating consequences upon the fortunes of the rest of the Harewoods and their family connections. We, all of us, are as poor as church mice, and our expectations are bound up in his Grace's bounty. Meagre enough it has been, and one can only hope that long before he is due to meet with his Maker—long before—he will have seen fit to have provided his grandnieces with the necessary to make decent marriages. Truly, Lydia," he remarked, turning to his wife, "your august relative is a most niggardly pinchpocket! I declare it would not make even a small dent in his great personal fortune—not say anything of the entail—if he would invite a grandniece or two out to Richmond Hill for a treat. I am thinking that if he deigned to notice them in that way—you understand, hold a rout or a ball for them, why, in that district alone, I dare say, they should make the acquaintance of any number of highly eligible young gentlemen who would value a connection to Grade. Does it not seem reasonable that there would

10

be little haggling over marriage portions with his Grace acting as *deus ex machina*, as it were?"

"Jonathan, when you begin to spout that horrid foreign nonsense, truly I do not know what to make of you," protested Mrs. Grantham.

"Oh, never mind. It is not important. I pray you will now let me peruse my correspondence. As for the duke and his housekeeper, I do not see that we can do ought to forestall his Grace, and we shall just have to wait until it happens. It is not beyond the realm of possibility that a female, other than that pitiable, browbeaten sister of his—oh, I assure you, my dear, I mean to imply nothing against her. But she was too sweet and too yielding before the tyrant that *he* is— well, I mean to say that a different sort of female just might make the old boy something human again—that is, if ever he was in the first place."

Satisfied that he had had his say, Mr. Grantham signaled a close to a profitless conversation by an ostentatious opening up of his journal and an equally deliberate positioning of it as a barrier between himself and his ladies.

Mrs. Grantham sighed, shrugged, and arose from the table. With a motion of her head, she signaled her daughter to join her, and they withdrew from the dining room arm in arm.

Mother and daughter were seated in the sewing room, each rummaging through a sewing basket to find the piece of work that they were finishing. At first one and then the other drew forth their particular piece, Mrs. Grantham remarked: "Phoebe, one has got to be practical. It is all very well to speak of love and romance when you are wealthy, but when you are poor, as are we, my dear, such ideas are sheer luxuries and unattainable except by chance—and you cannot afford to await upon Dame Fortune, or you will find yourself upon the shelf. You are seventeen years of age, and that is in your favor. Next year you will be eighteen, and your chances will be so much less favorable. I assure you, at twenty years of age and unwed and undowered, then are you on the shelf for good and all. At twenty, you can no longer say that you are still waiting for the right gentleman, for it will be believed by all, gentlemen included, that the right gentleman has long since passed you by. It is not my wish to dishearten you, child, but you have got to face your prospects honestly. With Aunt Sophia's demise, it is all over for us, and when I say us, I refer equally to all your girl cousins. They are all of them Harewoods, and all in the same fix as yourself. It was thought surely that Uncle Janus would provide, but he is old and alone and needs must find himself a housekeeper. Oh, why did all of you girls have to be so close in age! If only one of you was sufficiently old to have lost all hope of a household of her own, *she* could have become his housekeeper. She would have been old enough for the responsibility and could have devoted herself to him—and, best of all, she would have been blood of our blood—a Harewood!"

"Well, I, for one, could never find it in my heart to wish such a miserable fate on a relation of mine!" countered Phoebe, busy at her sewing.

"That will be quite enough out of you, young lady—and, furthermore, you are not thinking clearly. You could not be in your right mind if you would refuse an invitation to take up your residence on Richmond Hill. You will find only the wealthiest families there, the grounds are all in the latest fashion, and the houses veritable works of art. Surely you have noticed them. I admit the few times we have been on a visit to Uncle Janus, you were much too young to appreciate it all, but you saw how it was last week when we attended the obsequies for dear Aunt Sophia. How could you have not?"

"Well yes, Mama, it was all very grand, and I should dearly love just such a place for my own, but not if I must take his Grace with it. That is just too great a price to pay—"

Mr. Grantham had come striding into the room, holding a sealed letter in his hand. "I beg your pardons, ladies, but perhaps fortune has begun to smile upon us. I have here an epistle addressed to Miss Phoebe Harewood Grantham, and I'll wager you will never guess from whom it came. Shall I give you a hint?" he asked, smiling with evident satisfaction.

"A letter for me?" exclaimed Phoebe in the greatest surprise.

"Oh, Jonathan, do not tease us, I pray! If it be good news tell us at once, for I do declare that we are in need of some at this moment!"

Mr. Grantham made a flourish and presented the letter to his daughter. "It is for you, my dear, and so I leave it to you to be the first to savor its contents. I am sure it cannot be anything but the best of tidings for us."

Eagerly, Phoebe snatched the letter from her father's hand and quickly slipped her hand under the heavy wax seal to break it open, but she paused and stared at it.

"Oh no!" she cried. "What on earth can be so marvellous in it? It is merely come from Richmond Hill. I daresay it is some inconsequential note from his Grace's secretary."

13

"Nonsense, child! Since when has Grade seen fit to employ a secretary?—although with that crabbed fist of his, so like his nature, he could do worse than to employ at the least an amanuensis, I do declare. No, that is from his Grace's own hand and to you, Phoebe. Don't you understand the significance?"

"No, Papa, I do not, especially as I have yet to open and read what he has to say to me."

"Oh, child!" exclaimed Mrs. Grantham. "You disappoint me so! It is a most auspicious sign, for, by that letter you hold in your hands, his Grace, the Duke of Grade, is deigning to notice you! It is the answer to our prayers, I tell you!"

"But he is my great-uncle, Mama! What is so remarkable that he should notice me, his grandniece?"

"You are not his only grandniece. You have got to remember that your five Harewood cousins are his grandnieces as well, and not in my recollection has he ever communicated with a one of them. Believe me, if he had, I should have heard of it. It is a thing of the greatest pride for a mama to have her daughter noticed by a duke, even if he is a distant relation."

"Enough of this pointless chatter!" exclaimed Mr. Grantham. "I did not come arushing to you to listen to the obvious. Phoebe, my dear, I pray you will put an end to the suspense and open that letter. I am sure we all must be interested to learn what has occasioned your great-uncle to unbend to you."

Phoebe began to fumble with the letter.

All impatience, Mrs. Grantham reached for it, exclaiming: "Here, let me have it! It will be lunchtime before ever *you* get it open."

"Mrs. Grantham, let your daughter be and contain yourself, I pray," Mr. Grantham admonished his wife.

By that time, Phoebe had gotten the letter open

14

and was reading it, an expression of distaste beginning to appear on her face.

She looked up and said: "Well, if that is Uncle Janus's idea of notice, I am far better off without it!"

"What do you mean?" demanded Mrs. Grantham, snatching the letter out of her daughter's hand and running her eyes over it.

She looked up from it and exclaimed: "What nonsense are you speaking, child? This is beyond our greatest hopes for you!"

Highly wroth, she turned to her husband and handed the note to him, saying: "Grade is inviting Phoebe to come stay with him at Richmond Hill for some weeks. Can you imagine the good fortune in that? And our precious daughter is acting as though it was to his seat in Cornwall. Just look at her! Did you ever in your life witness such a sour expression in the face of such an excellent prospect?"

Mr. Grantham was studying the note and nodding. "Of course she must go. This is in the nature of a command. The old gentleman comes as close to demanding her presence as manners will permit."

"Of course she must go—and with a better expression on her visage—"

"Well, I shall not!" retorted Phoebe. "I'd rather die than have to spend even a day in his Grace's miserable presence!"

Mr. Grantham, very much irked, retorted: "Young lady, none of your insolence! You are going and there's an end to it! Now sit yourself down and indite a proper acceptance to his Grace, and then begin at once to pack! Let me see, he says here he expects you to be with him by month's end. Now, that should give you plenty of time, I am sure, to prepare."

"Oh, is that what he says?" exclaimed Mrs. Grantham. "But that is never enough time!"

"Of course it is, Lydia!" said Mr. Grantham, vexed. "What, has Phoebe so many affairs to settle before she departs? I am sure it is just a matter of tossing a few things in a bag and going off."

"Oh, you men! Of course it is not that simple! Our daughter is going to make her appearance at Richmond Hill! Do you wish his Grace to be ashamed of her? She has got to take along with her a deal more than just a few things. After all, he is bound to give a party in her honor, and, I assure you, she has not a thing to wear upon such a grand occasion. If she is to make any appearance at all, I shall need at least one hundred and fifty pounds to see her decently clothed."

"At least? cried Mr. Grantham in tortured tones. "What have we here? A society miss? Phoebe is not going to be presented at court! She is merely going to stay with a dear great-uncle who has a deep affection for her. Let *him* buy her what she needs. One hundred and fifty pounds would not lighten his pockets in the least; whereas such a sum is bound to make mine disappear, I tell you!"

Phoebe, at the height of her indignation and at the depth of her wisdom, chose that moment to say, in a most impertinent tone: "You need have no concern about what I am going to wear at Richmond Hill, for the fact of the matter is that I am not going there!"

"Jonathan, I implore you! Speak to your daughter!"

"Young lady, you *are* going, and I'll not stand for your nonsense—"

"I beg your pardon, Papa. I did not mean to be impertinent; but I shall not go!" she ended up sulkily.

"Now that is more than enough out of you, Miss!

16

Go to your room! You are going to pay a visit to your kind, old great-uncle and like it if I have to carry you there kicking and screaming! Now, not another word, hear! Go to your room at once!" And he pointed with an imperious finger to the door.

Phoebe burst into tears, and, clapping her hands up to cover her face, she rushed from the room.

"I say! Whatever has got into the girl?" exclaimed Mr. Grantham.

"Now, dear, it is no manner of use to get too excited about it. Phoebe is a good girl, and she will come around. You will see. I will admit that a visit to Uncle Janus's is not a business of pleasure, but I shall take pains to explain to her why it is so necessary that the old crab is not to be crossed. She will understand for she is sensible."

"Well, I certainly hope so. If she were to appear upon his doorstep with an expression such as she has just shown us, it would be far better if she stayed as far away from Richmond Hill as she could."

"Truly, my dear, it is not as bad as it seems. Phoebe is but a product of these fast times. All the young people are taken with such a spirit of independence, I do declare, one is put to extraordinary pains to set them right. I know it was never so in my day. We were sedate and minded our elders. Today, sauciness is the style. Well, Phoebe may be as pert as she likes, but to Uncle Janus's she is going, and she will be as well-behaved as he could ask for before I am done with her. I shall go up to her now, and you may rely upon it, she will be putting a better face upon it by tomorrow. In fact, I have a notion to take her with me when I go to visit Sarah this afternoon."

17

"My sister? I did not think you and she got along so well."

"I cannot understand why you should say so. We have ever been friends. I do not see the harm in informing her of the good fortune that has come Phoebe's way."

"Oh, so that's it!" Mr. Grantham responded with a smile. "Nothing like a little envy to spark a friendship."

"Oh, Jonathan, how odious of you to say such a thing!" cried Mrs. Grantham, ruffling in indignation.

"I agree. I should have kept that remark to myself," he replied with a chuckle.

"Now that is snide indeed! I assure you I only wish to show Phoebe what a lucky girl she is. How better than to let her see the awe and disappointment in her cousin's eyes at the news. I assure you that will make up her mind for her quickly enough."

"My dear, I do not admire the spirit of this particular endeavor of yours, but I am heartily in accord with its purpose. In fact, I must compliment you on your resourcefulness. I should never have thought of it."

"Well, of course you would not have. Men just are not very clever at this sort of business."

She left the sitting room, and Mr. Grantham sat back and chuckled.

Chapter II

Mr. Grantham had every confidence in his wife's ability to deal with his daughter, and, that afternoon, he cheerfully went off to spend the day with a neighbor for a few hours of masculine conversation, something he had come to need more and more as his only child came to be more and more of a woman with each passing year.

Upon his return to the bosom of his family, he was devastated to discover that for once his helpmate had failed him, so woefully had she failed him that no sooner had he stepped foot inside the door but she was on him, demanding that he speak with his unregenerate offspring.

"But, my dear, did you never get her to go with you to my sister's? You assured me that it was a most excellent way of convincing her."

"And surely it was but for that odious old relation of mine! You will never guess what Uncle Janus has gone and done!"

"I am sure you are right. I haven't an inkling."

"Oh, you will never believe it! He has gone and invited Philomena just as he has invited Phoebe. Can you imagine the nerve of that monster?"

"No, I cannot. It is beyond imagination that anyone in his right mind would wish to put himself through

19

such an ordeal. Phoebe and Philomena, too? Madam, I stand in awe of your venerable relative."

"Jonathan Grantham, I assure you this is not a subject for levity—and there is more, and it is even worse than you have already heard," she said, the expression on her face one of determination to shock her husband.

He looked at her and frowned. "Surely there can be nothing worse—unless he elected to gather to his avuncular bosom all five of his nieces at the same time."

"Exactly! Philomena's letter was a duplicate of Phoebe's. Now what do you think of that?"

"I think his Grace is far gone in senility and bow to my daughter's judgement for once. I can see no point to her joining the crush—"

"How can you say such a thing?" wailed Mrs. Grantham, in loud protest. "It is more important than ever that she go! Don't you see? Uncle Janus is softening. He is lonely and needs must gather his descendants—whom he has most shamefully neglected all these years—he must gather them to him to help light his declining years—"

"Now, just a moment, Lydia! Uncle Janus is no young rooster, it is true, but I hope my declining years will come to find me in as good a shape as his Grace. What nonsense is this? I can see his inviting all of his nieces, one at a time, but all together? It just does not make sense to me. Consider that he could never stand a one of them at any age, not to say that he was ever overly tolerant of any of his relations, and you are forced to conclude it has got to be a strange business he has in mind."

"Oh for heaven's sake, Jonathan! That is not at all to the point! If Uncle Janus should be considering a revision of his will, would not we look the fools to have kept Phoebe from him at such an important time?"

"And, madam, exactly how do you come by that precious bit of information, may I inquire?"

"What difference whether it be true or not! The fact of the matter is that the idea is not impossible, and we cannot risk Phoebe's being overlooked if it should prove to be so. And if it is not, what have we lost? The child is in need of decent clothing anyway. This is as good an excuse as any to provide them, I say."

Mr. Grantham appeared to be undecided.

Mrs. Grantham pressed home the attack. "Jonathan, I have all sympathy for Phoebe in this hour of trial. Uncle Janus is a most unpleasant curmudgeon in his best days, I will admit; but the girl does have a duty to him as he is the head of her family. Her not going can only be seen as a slight to his Grace and can do none of us the least good in his eyes. If she obeys his summons, at worst she will suffer an unpleasant week or two, a very small price to pay to avoid the consequences of her not going off to Richmond Hill."

Mr. Grantham smiled sourly. "For once, my dear, I find your logic irrefutable—but only because we happen to be so hard pressed to provide for our daughter's future. I assure you, had I the wherewithal, I should not raise a finger to insist upon Phoebe's attendance at Richmond Hill. It is most humiliating to know that one has no choice."

Mrs. Grantham smiled soothingly. "Of course, my dear, I do understand. As you have just pointed out, beggars cannot be choosers."

He bristled and glared at her. "That was not precisely what I meant," he retorted and stormed out of the room.

Phoebe's countenance was set in a stubborn mold as she leaned against her bedpost and seethed. She was determined that she would never comply with her mother's demand that she go off to visit with the Duke of Grade. She could not stand Uncle Janus! He was a very ancient gentleman, but she did not hold that against his Grace. There were a fair number of old gentlemen in the neighborhood who were the most pleasant and the kindliest of men and with whom she had many a jolly conversation. Uncle Janus was never anything at all like them.

Uncle Janus did not resemble them in the least. His deep-set eyes had such a piercing glance that one could never be at ease in his presence, and his thin lips never smiled. The few times that she had been to see him with her parents, never once had he smiled. If ever his mouth relaxed, it was into a sneer or some expression as unpleasant. His Grace was ever short with young people, as though they were never worth his bother to set them in their place—and truly he had no need to take any great pains, for one thrust of his glance had always been sufficient to deprive her of the power of speech. How could anyone expect her to welcome an opportunity to spend even a day with such a strange specimen, however high his rank?

Phoebe had never a doubt that her revulsion for her great-uncle was based on all good reason and that, if only her parents would consider it in that light, they would never persist in forcing her to go out to Richmond Hill. But deep within her heart, she had the feeling that her fate had been sealed from the moment that the wax upon the letter had given way under her thumb, that, willy-nilly, out to Uncle Janus's she was bound to journey.

The awful prospect was bound to be unalterable, for she had chatted with her cousin, Philomena, and all that had ensued with her own parents had already occurred with Philomena's the marks on her cousin's cheeks attesting to that young lady's tearful defeat. Yes, that was a consolation. She would have Philomena as partner in her misery, and, undoubtedly, Harriette, Jane, and Fredericka as well—the others of her Harewood cousins.

Come to think of it, it might not be all that bad after all. Five young ladies ought to be able to divert themselves in the beautiful environs of Richmond Hill despite the demands that a crotchety old great-uncle might see fit to put upon them. Besides, Uncle Janus was so very old by this time, it would not be surprising if he spent practically all of his days drowsing away in a rocking chair.

The storm in her face began to clear. Yes, she thought, the visit was bound to be inevitable. Why not consider the brighter side of the matter? And there was truly a brighter side. There were the new clothes to be bought, and from London, too, which meant a shopping trip in to the city. That was a most excellent prospect. And the journey itself across the Thames and through Surrey would be just long enough to enjoy without becoming a boring ordeal. And then there would be the meeting with her cousins, the three latter whom she so rarely ever saw, so scattered as the Harewoods were, in and about the great city and its outlying reaches.

It was not impossible that his Grace might even hold a rout in their honor—after all, he had to do something with five young ladies—what better than to

23

give a party? And all the beaux of Richmond would attend—and there she would be dressed to the nines in all her new-bought London finery—

It is no wonder that when Mrs. Grantham came up to Phoebe's room to lay the law down to her, she was quite taken aback to discover that her daughter had not only turned obedient to her wish, but was actually evincing some small signs of enthusiasm for her approaching visit to the residence of the Duke of Grade.

Up until the day the twin letters arrived, Phoebe and Philomena had had little to say and even less to do with each other, and it was not because they lived so far apart either. As a matter of fact, the small estates each of their gentleman fathers was in possession of were situated not more than four miles from each other. It was just that the two families moved in somewhat different circles and met only upon the occasion of rare family functions and the more frequent doings in and about their rather rural neighborhood.

But the imminence of having to contend with the Great Ogre of Richmond, as the girls delighted in calling his Grace, acted to unite them in a way that even the family tie could not, and they were now frequently to be seen calling at each other's homes and uniting their heads in councils of war. Cool cousins before, now in the face of the common enemy, they quickly became bosom companions.

One afternoon, all their shopping done and with nothing to do but wait for their day of departure to arrive, they were seated in the garden together before Phoebe's home.

"Papa thinks it is an excellent idea for us to go

down to Richmond together, Philomena. He says it will save expense and will save at least one of our papas the exertion. I dare say they will draw straws to see which one of them must drive us. I do declare, if it were not for my mama, I should never have to go. I am sure papa agrees with mama only because she insists upon it."

"I well understand, for it is the same at my house. Well," she sighed, "there is naught we can do but make the best of it. But why did his Grace have to do it?"

"What?" asked Phoebe. "Do you know what all this is in aide of?"

"No, I have not a smidgin of an idea. Do you?"

"Well no, I do not, but I thought from your remark that you did and were wondering why he had gone to the trouble."

"Well, I am wondering about that, but not because I know what the old ogre has got up his sleeve. I say, Phoebe, do you think the old gentleman is going dotty in his old age and has a wish to do something nice for his nieces before it is too late?"

Phoebe frowned as she turned the idea over in her mind. "No, I cannot imagine Uncle Janus as ever being dotty." She burst into merry laughter as a thought struck her. "I do mean ever! Can you imagine the sort of baby Uncle Janus was? Oh, his nurse must have been terrified half out of her wits of him! No, Uncle Janus, I am sure, never was the least bit mild and is never like to be."

"Oh, I guess you are right," remarked Philomena disconsolately. "But then why is he going to all this trouble? Mama is quite assured that all our cousins have been invited, too—and I will admit that that makes it a deal easier to bear—But, oh, what if it had been just me!—or you! How awful for us! To have to stay with him for even a week must make it seem like a year!"

Phoebe gave vent to an exaggerated shudder. "Ohooh! It does not bear thinking on! I should much rather talk about our new clothes. That is one thing pleasant that has come to us as a result of his Grace's invitation. You know, for that we do owe him some thanks. I should not have had anything new until spring but for Uncle Janus."

Philomena giggled. "I ought not to say it, but Mama was in such a rush to fit me out, one would have thought I had only rags to my name. She took me in to *Louise* and—"

"Oh, yes, I know that shop. We went to *Madame Laurent*. Mama swears by her! And she does have the loveliest things! And *expensive*? My dear, when poor Papa gets the bill, he is sure to have a fit!"

Philomena chortled: "Mine, too! I venture to say that if it should arrive before we set out, I would not put it past my papa to send it all back and never let me go."

"Well, my papa will send everything back, including his daughter as well, I'll be bound!"

Both girls laughed at the imagined rage of their out-at-the-pocket papas and the fuss they were bound to raise.

A very serious expression appeared upon Phoebe's face as she said: "Well, it will serve them right! Had they the least paternal feeling, they would never allow their daughters to be packed off to the Great Ogre of Richmond. It is only fair that, if they send us upon such a dire errand, they pay for our discomfort—although *I* think it should be Uncle Janus who should pay. He it is who is the cause of it all!" she ended indignantly.

"Oh!" wailed Philomena. "I do so wish that we knew why Uncle Janus asked for us to come!"

And so their conversation began for the tenth time to repeat its unvarying refrain.

They worried at the thought for a few minutes like a pair of puppy dogs with a bone too great in size for them and then let the matter drop in favor of further discussion of the impending visit.

Asked Phoebe: "I have not seen either Fredericka or Harriette or Jane in years! What are they like, do you think?"

"Oh, well, I have not seen any of them either, but my mother has heard that Fredericka is a positive beauty! I do not think I am going to like her."

"What more does your mother have to say about her?"

"Oh, just that she has more beaux than you can count—all that sort of thing. It is only to be expected."

"I dare say she will be the apple in his Grace's eye. It is always like that," remarked Phoebe, discontentedly.

"So much the better for the rest of us, I should think. Let her wait upon his Grace. I am sure that we can find better things to do," returned Philomena.

"I just hope that there are other things to do there, even if not better. It appears to me that it will be a bore. Perhaps Jane and Harriette will be fun, do you think?"

"I do not know what to think. Do you realize that his Grace has not said for how long we shall be required to abide with him?"

"Oh, I do not think it will be overlong. Uncle Janus is not long on abiding folk of any sort, much less young people. No, I do not think we need concern ourselves with that. A few days and he will have had enough of us, I do not doubt."

"Actually, Phoebe, our stay with him cannot be too short for me. I—I fear Uncle Janus. One would think he was a Czar of Russia the way he behaves. I know even my parents are not comfortable in his presence. Oh, can you just imagine how poor Aunt Sophia must have suffered under his tyranny?"

"Well, everyone says she did—but, now that I think of it, I am not so sure. The few times that I recall, I do not seem to remember that she was in any great difficulty with his Grace."

"Oh, then you could never have seen what I did!" exclaimed Philomena in a voice of horror. "I saw him once call her all sorts of nasty names, he even ordered her out of the room for daring to contradict him. It was ever so humiliating. I blush at the mere recollection."

Phoebe shook her head. "Oh, that is nothing. I have seen him treat her as though she were a dog, but the thing I am getting at is that she did not seem to mind. She truly did not seem to mind him at *all!*"

"Really! Just because she was inured to it after all those years of miserable treatment at his hands is no call for declaring that she did not mind it!" argued Philomena.

"Not it—him! That is what I am getting at, don't you see? Tell me, when his Grace ordered her out of the room, did she obey him?"

"No, she did not, and I thought she was awfully brave to defy him so, too."

"That is what I thought. I observed that through all his vituperation, Aunt Sophia merely stood by patiently with her eyebrows on high, waiting for him to

28

finish, like a governess, sort of, with an unruly child. You know what I mean. When the child is in a temper, but not enough to deserve a spanking?"

"Oh, how you talk, Phoebe! Spank Uncle Janus? Spank his Grace, the Duke of Grade? What rubbish is that? For all his years, it would take a sizable fellow to down him! Spank Uncle Janus? That is a fanciful thought if I ever heard one!"

"Oh, you are taking me too literally, and anyway, I am only speaking of the look upon Aunt Sophia's countenance—oh, forget I ever said it! It is not making any sense."

"I should say it isn't!" agreed Philomena, a bit indignantly. She eyed her cousin for a while, and then she asked: "What are you thinking of?"

"I am thinking that, since we have got to put up with his Grace, perhaps Aunt Sophia's way is not to be overlooked."

Philomena stood up. She was quite annoyed now. "Really, Phoebe, what a thing to say! Poor Aunt Sophia! How can you believe that she was anything but put upon! I shall be content if his Grace does not even *notice* me! I should think we are to be thankful that Fredericka will be there and take his eye. I do not envy her her prettiness in that case."

Rising, Phoebe said: "I hope you are right. Even if Aunt Sophia did have a way with Uncle Janus, it was surely not pleasant at best for her."

"Well, I am not looking forward to Richmond Hill."

"Nor am I!"

Chapter III

THEY TRAVELED by post chaise. Mr. Grantham was the parent who escorted the two young ladies to Pickering Hall, the residence of the Duke of Grade. The three of them were reasonably comfortable on the wide seat of the chaise and not under any great strain over the less than forty miles of roads stretching between their homes near Stevenage village and the palatial estates of Richmond. Their baggage had been sent on by carter before them, and so the chaise was able to bowl along at close to ten miles an hour.

Mr. Grantham took his duty a deal more seriously than either of the young ladies cared for, and they listened to his admonitions with but half an ear each. Mr. Grantham, pointing out more than once his relationship as both father and uncle respectively to his charges, was at great pains to stress the good fortune that they were about to enjoy. Not very many young ladies could boast of a duke for a relative, and it must behoove them to be on their best behaviour for as long as his Grace condescended to shower his favor upon them. They were to be perfect ladies at every moment and true Harewoods. He hoped they would make him proud, he hoped they would make Mr. Mellor, Philomena's father, proud, and most of all, he devoutly wished that the both of them would make his Grace, the Duke, proud.

Phoebe devoutly wished her papa would not prose on so. The apprehension aroused by the prospect of what lay before them at the end of the journey was all she cared to devote her thinking to, and her parent's insistence upon reviewing for them the rules of proper conduct for young ladies, so reminiscent of the long dreary hours she had had to spend under Mrs. Thatcher's tutelage, was not in the least comforting, nor did it make the journey any less of a trial.

It was a conscientious, but heartless, postboy they had, and, had there been a load of luggage aboard, one could be justified in wondering how the poor beasts managed such a killing pace mile after mile; but, as none of the passengers were at all knowledgeable concerning the care and management of horseflesh, they could only be pleased that the trip would be accomplished in good time.

At last, the postboy began to pull in the horses and the chaise slowed to a less reckless pace as they came into the winding roads ascending the modest rise just over the Thames to the southwest of London. The adornment of Richmond Hill quite took the young ladies' breath. One great estate after another passed in review before their admiring gaze, and Mr. Grantham, somewhat winded from his lengthy discourse, relapsed into silence, unable to compete for their attention.

Phoebe was particularly enthralled. It seemed to her that a whole lifetime had passed since she had last been in the neighborhood on a visit to her greatuncle. She had been much too young to appreciate the impressive beauty of the place then, so that it was actually like seeing it all for the first time now.

One velvety lawn succeeded another, each spreading like great green aprons up to mansions and cottages ornée, all of whose construction had been executed to a gemlike perfection. Hedges, shrubs, and trees were manicured and barbered into shapes that nature had never intended and added such a romantic touch to the settings as to tug at her heart with longing to someday have such beauty for her own. She was at pains to recall exactly what Pickering Hall's style was and how its grounds were laid out, but, for the life of her, she could not conjure up a picture of the place in her mind. All that would come back to her was the overpowering figure of the duke. It quite filled her mind to the exclusion of any other impression of the Hall and only added to the apprehension that was mounting within her breast as every step of the horses brought her nearer to her journey's end. She was sure that Pickering Hall could not be anything like the charming villas, surrounded by fountains and exquisite statuary, appearing on every side.

But she was wrong. The carriage turned into a short approach and passed through a pair of immense, ornately worked wrought-iron gates, mounted below a soaring archway, and then ran along a broad roadway, bisecting a vast rolling lawn, dotted here and there with artfully arranged groupings of trees and shrubs arranged about a marble pavilion or a fountain or just a small bed of gloriously hued flowers.

"Gad! The money that man spends on fripperies he cannot even care about!" exclaimed Mr. Grantham. "I daresay we could live in the highest style for years on the tin buried in these grounds of his."

"Indeed, Papa, they are very beautiful," remarked Phoebe, somewhat subdued.

"Hmph! They ought to be, considering the small army he employs to maintain them. Ah, yes, speaking of servants, I wonder if he has got a new housekeeper yet. Imagine all of this winding up in the lap of some passing female with not a drop of Harewood in her!"

"Do you think Uncle Janus has already got one?" asked Phoebe.

"I am sure I have not the faintest notion. Of course, the old gentleman would never think to consult his relations on so important a matter. We are all of us far too poor to be worthy of such recognition," he said bitterly.

"But, Papa, I had always thought that we live in comfort, and, certainly, you have the respect of our neighbors—"

"Child, consider that you are a relation to a duke of England. Somewhere back in your lineage, the family was very close to royalty, and the blood of a king of England flows through your veins. Does that not warrant something greater than mere comfort, something greater than mere respect?"

"But, Papa, *you* are not a Harewood—"

"What has that to say to anything! Your mother is and should be accorded a greater dignity than merely that of poor relation to the Duke of Grade."

"But all of the other Harewoods fare little better than we do if at all," she pointed out.

"Of course, and so they share with us the same distinction. Grade is probably just about the wealthiest man in the land and, certainly, the only man of wealth to be able to claim that everyone of his relations is a poor one."

The sardonic expression upon her father's face, as

34

he gave vent to his thoughts, Phoebe found particularly disquieting, and it made no improvement in the feeling, akin to dread, that was flourishing in her breast with the journey so close to its termination. She glanced at Philomena and saw in her face a reflection of her own anxieties. It had always been a matter of family pride that the Harewoods were connected with the Duke of Grade, and that he was excessively wealthy only enhanced the connection. That somehow it worked to humble rather than exalt their station in life, she had not realized until this very moment. The expression of resentment upon her father's countenance amply attested to the fact, and the revelation could not have come to her at a more inopportune moment, a moment when she was devoting all of her thoughts to the problem of coping with his Grace. It was eminently clear to her that if her father felt the way he did, how very less secure must she be in the presence of that awful peer, her relative the duke.

But time for such reflections was past. The chaise drew up before the Hall and came to a stop. They had arrived.

Oh yes! Pickering Hall was most certainly right up with the best of the architectural creations displayed on Richmond Hill, thought Phoebe as she stepped down from the carriage and gazed up and about at the great mansion, Philomena close at her side.

She remembered the plum-red brick expanse margined at the many corners with gray stone dressings and broken up at regular intervals by tall, multipaned windows.

The great doorway, yawning under a massive carved lintel, was particularly uninviting, she thought, and she experienced the greatest reluctance to mount the wide stairs leading up to it.

Mr. Grantham was part way up when he stopped and looked back down.

"I say, ladies, what in heaven's name are you waiting for?"

She felt a tug at her sleeve, and Philomena said: "Phoebe! Your father awaits us!"

With leaden limbs she began to mount the stairs. Mr. Grantham turned and administered some authoritative raps upon the portal with the heavy, gleaming brass knocker.

By the time the girls had reached his side, the door was swinging open. Phoebe was disappointed not to hear it squeak. She was sure it ought to, to go with her dreary mood.

A butler issued forth and, making a little bow, said: "Ah, Mr. Grantham, so good of you to come."

He regarded each young lady in turn and then looked to Mr. Grantham. "I am sure we have both Miss Grantham and Miss Mellor here, but, beyond that they are true Harewoods, I cannot distinguish between them."

"Of course, Addington," and Mr. Grantham, disturbed at the butler's manner, proceeded to introduce his daughter and his niece.

"Thank you, sir. His Grace thanks you for your kindness in carrying the ladies to Pickering Hall and would not think of detaining you further."

"Oh I say!" exclaimed Mr. Grantham taken aback. "Er—I had hoped to exchange a word or two with his Grace ere I returned home."

"Ah yes, Mr. Grantham. But I am instructed to inform you that his Grace is not disposed to make an appearance at this time and would take it as a great favor if you did not press for an audience with him."

Mr. Grantham blinked. "Well, no, I shall hardly in-

36

sist upon it. I mean to say, I had just hoped to make inquiry into his Grace's health and commend these young ladies to his protection."

"Of course, Mr. Grantham, and I am authorized to assure you, in his Grace's name, that they shall be cared for and cherished as though they were his own daughters. So you see, sir, there is not the slightest need for you to tarry longer. You have a long journey home if you expect to be back in Stevenage by nightfall."

"Hmmm. Yes, of course."

Looking quite discomfited, Mr. Grantham turned to the girls and said: "Well, my dears, I shall leave you with Addington. Now, do behave yourselves and mind your manners before his Grace."

He stooped and kissed each young lady good-bye. Then he proceeded down the stairs to the waiting chaise. He turned and waved.

"Remember now! Do not forget to write a frequent letter to your mothers. I am sure his Grace will not object to franking them for you."

He stepped into the carriage and was driven away.

Addington stood quietly by while the girls waved and watched as the carriage disappeared down the great drive.

Addington held the door open, and the young ladies entered the great house.

"You will meet with his Grace shortly before dinner. I will have you shown to your rooms where you can refresh yourselves and change. A maid has been assigned to each of you, and your things have been placed in your rooms. Miss Fredericka, Miss Harriette, and Miss Jane arrived earlier, and you will find them in the music room when you are ready to come down. His Grace requests that you do not wander about the house or the grounds on this your first day. There will be plenty of time for that later. In fact, he has a wish that you all will make it your business to become well-acquainted with the estate during your stay with him. The fact of the mattter is that one can lose oneself quite easily in the ramifications of this structure, and it would be a bit of a bother to have to turn out the household to find you, don't you see," he ended with a little laugh.

Phoebe was relieved to hear that the duke was not in the immediate offing, and so she could be at ease for another hour or two. The idea of having to meet with him without the protecting presence of her father had been daunting, to say the least. And, too, it would be much easier to meet with him as one of a group of cousins than with only Philomena at her side.

At Addington's signal, two maids made their appearance, and the young ladies were conducted upstairs to the guest chambers they were to occupy.

Phoebe's maid, without a word, opened a door off the hall, and Phoebe, all in a trance over the sumptuous decor that greeted her eyes at every step of the way through the mansion, entered the rooms she was to live in for who knew how long.

She came to a stop just within the door and looked about, quite overwhelmed. Never before had she seen anything so grand. Up until this moment her concept of extravagant wealth had been completely introspective. To be wealthy had meant to be free from care, to be completely independent, to never have to make do. But here before her very eyes was a meaning of riches that she had not imagined. Here before her eyes the physical trappings of excessive affluence were gloriously displayed.

Her tiny room at home had had all the conveniences a young lady could require but—just looking about at the great tester, hung with heavy draperies, the exquisitely graceful furniture, obviously from the hands of the most expert cabinetmakers, the soft, lush oriental rug under her feet and—why she was even to have her very own fireplace!

She rushed over to the hearth and stood before it, staring at the great mantelpiece carved all over with leaves and acorns.

"The rooms tend to be dampish, Miss Grantham, and a small fire is required. If it is too hot—"

"No, no, it is quite all right, Buckle. I—I was just admiring the very handsome mantelpiece."

"Oh yes, Miss. There be even finer; aye, and in rooms we never use."

"Heavens! Pickering Hall must be even larger than one might suspect!" exclaimed Phoebe, going over to the bed. She drew aside the curtains and sat down upon it. "Oh!" she exclaimed gleefully. "It is so marvellously soft, I am sure I could drop off in an instant."

She laid herself down upon it and closed her eyes. It was as though the bed were alive to her needs, and she felt the tension within her drain away. It was a great feeling of ease and comfort. She smiled and a curtain drifted down. Her thoughts began to wander—and she was asleep.

"Miss Grantham! Miss Grantham!"

An unfamiliar voice sounded in Phoebe's ear, as a hand gently shook her awake.

"Miss Grantham! Miss Grantham! It is getting on

39

towards dinnertime! You must change! You cannot keep his Grace waiting!"

At the words "his Grace" Phoebe came awake at once. She sat up on the bed and looked around.

Buckle stepped back as her charge smiled and stretched.

"Oh, Buckle, never have I slept in anything so soft and comfortable!"

"Miss Phoebe, it is getting late and his Grace insists on promptness."

Phoebe made a face and slipped from the bed. Except that her shoes had been removed, she was still in the same garb in which she had come.

At once Buckle began to help her out of her things.

"What shall I wear? Does his Grace require formal dress?"

Buckle frowned. "I have gone through your things, and I daresay we can make do with something. One never knows what his Grace wishes. He is a most changeable person—but perhaps you know that, Miss."

"Well, I know he is not the most pleasant sort of person, and I cannot say that I am looking forward with any great enthusiasm to dining with him. Tell me, how do you find his Grace? I have not seen him in some five years, and then he quite frightened me— not that he paid the least attention to me then."

"Oh, Miss Phoebe, it is not for me to comment upon the likes of such a great gentleman! His Grace is most generous, I assure you."

"How long have you been a member of his household?"

Buckle had freed Phoebe of her outer garments and was now assisting her into what the young lady knew to be her finest gown. It spoke volumes to her

40

of what her great-uncle required in terms of dress and ceremony.

"I have been with his Grace almost three years, but truly it was Lady Sophia who managed us all. Ah, now, there was a fine lady. His Grace misses her, I'll be bound. The household has not been the same since her passing."

"Was she happy here? It seemed to me his Grace was quite harsh with her."

Buckle chuckled. "Oh, his Grace is harsh with all. Her ladyship never minded his manner. Ah, she was a dear lady."

"She did not fear his Grace, did she?"

"Lawks no, child! His Grace was forever firing of everyone—I, myself, have been given the sack at least three times—or was it two? I venture to say that his Grace would have been hard put to keep any servants at all if her ladyship had not come between him and the help. Why, do you know that since her passing a footman, a groom, and two maids have been sent packing? And for no great thing, either. Lady Sophia would never have permitted it! Oh, the Hall is a poor place for her removal! It is never the same. I do not suppose any of us have expectations of remaining with his Grace any great length of time. He is not a man to be satisfied, and when he is not satisfied, someone is bound to get the sack. I dare say it will be my turn any day now."

Phoebe was deep in thought and paying little attention to Buckle's efforts with her garments, allowing herself to be turned and nudged as Buckle found it necessary.

Said Buckle: "I beg your pardon, Miss Phoebe, for speaking out so against his Grace, but it cannot make the least difference. If you should relate to him this

41

conversation, I shall be discharged upon the spot, but then I should have been discharged tomorrow or the next day, I do not doubt, and for something never so bad as this."

"It is quite all right, Buckle. I thank you for your frankness. From what you have said, it is my guess that I shall be sent packing as soon, grandniece or no—and I'll not be sorry for it either!"

Following Buckle's directions, Phoebe descended to the ground floor and found her way to the small salon next to the dining hall. She was the last one to arrive, and her four cousins immediately stared at her intently.

At a glance, Phoebe could recognize Fredericka, despite the fact it had been long years since she had last seen her. Certainly the prettiest of them all, that young lady, just by the way she sat in her chair, seemed to proclaim herself queen of this little assembly, and it appeared to Phoebe that no one of them was about to deny it.

"Good evening, Cousins. It is so nice to be able to renew our acquaintance with each other," she said with a smile as she sat herself down.

Harriette replied: "Indeed, Cousin, but one could have wished it had occurred under happier circumstances."

Phoebe smiled in agreement and would have answered, but Fredericka interposed: "Really, Harriette, I do not know what you mean. I cannot imagine a happier circumstance than for us to meet together under the roof of dear Uncle Janus."

Asked Phoebe: "Have you been with Uncle Janus much before this?"

"Oh, not all that much, but enough to be so very

42

pleased that he has at last decided to notice us, his grandnieces, who are so devoted to him."

Snapped Harriette: "Speak for yourself, Frederickal *I* am not devoted to his Grace."

Fredericka reared up in her seat. "The illustrious head of the Harewoods and you are not devoted to his Grace? How very shocking of you! I do declare it borders on treason to the family—not to mention the hypocrisy of your having accepted of his Grace's generous hospitality!"

Harriette laughed sardonically as she retorted: "I never did! It was my parents who accepted and forced me to come! *That* is not hypocrisy! That is merely opportunism!"

"Oh, mercy!" cried Fredericka. "How very indelicate of you to say so!"

Harriette turned to the others. "I bid you speak, my Cousins, and say how very happy you all are to be here at Pickering Hall. I would know who truly are the hypocrites amongst us. You, Jane, pray inform us of *your* delight in being here under Uncle Janus's roof!"

Jane blushed and licked her lips. "I—I am sure that I do not find it in the least objectionable. My parents said I should not."

"Oh, mercy!" exclaimed Harriette, mocking Fredericka's manner. "How very biddable in you! You, Philomena, how was it with you? Are you, too, as delighted as Fredericka at finding yourself here, and are you so very biddable, too?"

Philomena had all the appearance of a frightened bird. She glanced in appeal at Phoebe.

Phoebe chuckled loudly and retorted: "Dearest Harriette, from whence comes your high nose? You are here along with us and, obviously, are not so very

43

pleased with it. One can only conclude, therefore, that you are, at least, as biddable as are all of us—with the exception, that is, of dear, sweet Fredericka, the Belle of the Harewoods."

Harriette scowled and sat back while Fredericka beamed upon Phoebe.

"Split me! If we have not got us a female wit amongst us!" exclaimed a harsh voice from the doorway. "Pah! I do detest 'em!"

As one, all the young ladies' heads turned to the doorway.

With both hands resting upon the head of his cane, the Duke of Grade stood there surveying his young relations, a sneer distorting his lips.

Phoebe felt a surge of resentment fill her breast and, in a fit of contrariness, held her seat, while the others, led by Fredericka, arose to do obeisance to his Grace.

Fredericka declared: "Your Grace does too much honor to his humble nieces."

The duke conferred a sour look upon her and strode over to stand before Phoebe. He had no more need of a cane than any of the young ladies.

"It would appear to me, Fredericka, that you do not speak for all of your cousins. This young lady appears to have some reservations. You are Grantham's girl, are you not?"

"Yes, your Grace."

"Have you never been instructed in manners, Miss?"

"Indeed I have been, your Grace. I have been taught to rise out of respect for the aged—amongst others."

The duke stared at her for a moment, his eyes opening wide.

Phoebe, shocked to the quick at her own impertinence, quickly arose to her feet and sank into a deep curtsey before him.

She arose to find his Grace still staring at her, the sneer on his lips, if anything, more marked.

"I—I beg your pardon, your Grace."

Still he stared at her, one hand rising to finger his chin.

Phoebe, now mortified with shame, blushed. Murmuring, "I beg you will excuse me, your Grace," she started to move away.

"Young lady, stay where you are! I did not excuse you! Where do you think you are going?"

"I—I was sure that your Grace would request my absence after my offensive remark—"

"Offensive? Hardly! Flattering more like, and I compliment you, Phoebe, upon your quickness with words. I should be a veritable ogre were I to take offense at a remark so complimentary. Now, surely you do not take me for an ogre, do you?"

Phoebe shook her head in quick denial and blushed crimson.

The duke burst into laughter and winked at her. He nodded slyly. "Ah ha! I have found you out, my dear!"

Turning from her, he addressed the others. "Ladies, dinner is being served. Fredericka, as the reigning beauty, it shall be my pleasure to have you upon the right of me this first evening."

He held out his arm to her, and she, blushing prettily, accepted it and proceeded into the dining room, her head held high in appreciation of this signal honor paid to her by his Grace.

Through the meal, Phoebe, along with her cousins,

45

responded to his Grace's inquiries with regard to the states of health, activities, etc., of the several branches of the family. The duke seemed to be genuinely interested in the responses and was able to discuss with each their particular parents as well as brothers, where there were brothers, to such an extent that Phoebe was amazed. As far as she knew, there had never been any great contact between her parents and her great-uncle, yet he was marvellously well acquainted with them as well as some of the circumstances of their living. From the attitude of her cousins, it must have been the same for them, too.

As a result the meal progressed pleasantly enough, especially as it had been prepared with a high order of skill so that even the dullest of appetites must do it justice. The duke made a most gracious host to the young ladies, encouraging each of them to chat about their life at home. In a little while everyone was quite familiar with each other and on easy terms generally. His Grace appeared to be smiling approvingly on one and all, and it was a much more lighthearted group of ladies by the time of the last remove.

His Grace called for a light cordial to be served his nieces while he partook of some madeira. Very graciously, he asked the ladies for permission to smoke, which no one of them had a thought to deny, and then he called for their attention.

He lit up his cigar, puffed a bit, examined its end to see that it was burning properly, and began.

"My dear Nieces, it does this old man's heart great good to see you all here assembled under my roof. You are, all of you, and without exception, a joy to behold and no less than adornments upon the family tree of Harewood. I have called you all into my presence to see just exactly how well we Harewoods

46

have been doing for ourselves, and I must say we have been doing well indeed.

"I need hardly point out to you that I am the head of your family, and, in case you are not aware of it, I am quite its most affluent member as well. In fact, one might say that any Harewood treasure worthy of the name is in my possession. But, alas! The Harewoods have recently lost one of their jewels, nay, their diadem, and it—she—must be replaced! I speak of your late great-aunt, my sister, the Lady Sophia.

"Ah, I see looks of incomprehension upon your bright young faces. I shall speak more plainly.

"Ah, you are breathless with gratitude, I see. Good! greatly in need of tenderness and affection to ease my way through what is left of my life. Your Aunt Sophia was priceless to me in that respect, and I cannot do without her like. Now where, I ask you, am I to seek for someone to take her place at my side, to share with me my great wealth, to oversee the management of this great household, to make all provision that the Duke of Grade remains Grade? Where?

"Would you have me seek out some strange lady and set her up above my own kin? No, you would not!—"

Phoebe shifted uneasily in her chair, and the duke's sharp old eyes transfixed her. She froze.

"—The answer to my need is too obvious to require discussion. Where but amongst my charming and most obliging grandnieces. That is why I have summoned you all to spend a few weeks with me, your most gracious grand-uncle," he ended and looked about him, smiling at the girls.

They all of them were immobile with shock and each stricken visage was completely devoid of the least appreciation for what they had just heard.

47

"Ah, you are breathless with gratitude I see. Good! It is a fine beginning. Now, unfortunately, it is not practicable for me to have you all with me, much as you do wish it. No, five young ladies, for all their good intentions, for all their deep affection for their old uncle, would fill this great house to bursting with an activity I should not welcome, so it must come down to but one of you to succeed to Lady Sophia's high station."

This tremendous good news was greeted with such silent applause that only the sharp ears of his Grace could detect it.

"Excellent! Your unanimous approval heartens me to continue. At this present, I do not know you well enough. In the next few days it is my intention to remedy that lack so that I may discover which one of you is most worthy of the high honor. In order that my judgement be fair and the selection be equitable, it will be necessary for you to become acquainted with the requirements of the station and dignity of Mistress of Pickering Hall, and the only way that can be accomplished is to have each of you go about the place learning all that is done here and how it has been managed in the past. Now then, as you are all properly brought up young ladies, no doubt but that you are competent in the extreme with regard to matters of domestic economy. It follows that you will not experience any great difficulty in getting the hang of things in the Hall, for, except that it is an unusually large establishment, it could be your very own home—and so it shall be for that one young Harewood lady of the greatest competence.

"Starting tomorrow, then, you will each follow a schedule of getting acquainted with the various services and offices, a schedule that I have had Addington prepare. Your first week will be devoted to learning all you can as to how Pickering Hall is run.

"The following week, you will then begin to put what you have learned into practice, and I am sure that I shall have a most difficult time choosing amongst your various excellences. Nevertheless, I shall be a most impartial judge and see to it that only the most deserving of you achieves the station of Lady of the manor.

"In order to insure all fairness amongst you and that you do put forth your best efforts in the matter, know that any slacking will be summarily punished by a revocation of my hospitality to that misguided individual, and she shall be returned to her family with the mark of my displeasure made plain to her parents. I do not think more need be said upon that score? In fact, I do not think there need be any further discussion of the matter. I, Grade, have spoken. Good night, ladies, and pleasant dreams."

With that Janus, Duke of Grade, arose from the table and strode out of the room, his cane, quite forgotten, still resting against his chair.

It was just as well, for, as soon as the young ladies had caught their breath, the murmur of conversation that ensued had the sound of a beehive that had been jostled.

49

Chapter IV

PHOEBE HAD VISIONS of the old duke popping up everywhere during the week that was to follow and finding all manner of fault with everyone, but, in the event, it never happened. The duke left the young ladies strictly to their own devices and went about the Hall with never a word or glance at them. It was left to Addington to give to each young lady her study assignment for the day. In that way they did not have much time together for, while one was in the kitchen attending Cook, another might be out with the gardener inspecting young plants in the greenhouse.

Addington was not particularly happy about the arrangements. He resented having to distribute this bevy of ladies out and around the premises amongst his subordinates, for he knew that not much work would be accomplished with all the gabbing that was bound to go forward, not only between the ladies and the help, but amongst the help themselves after the ladies had moved on to their next post of study.

What was even worse to his mind was the nature of the remarks it was his pleasure to overhear. The Harewood ladies were, to begin with, something less than competent in matters of domestic economy. All that they had any experience of were maids and the most primitive culinary practice. René, the chef, made vociferous complaint that their French was miserable and they could not understand a word of his menus. The footmen and the grooms and even he, Addington himself, were great curiosities to them. That is what one gets when one has so many poor relations—not one of them could qualify for the menial position of second upstairs maid, he thought. And when he contemplated the horror of one of these ladies becoming mistress of the household over him, his pink wattles quivered in indignation.

As for the girls themselves, without exception, they each of them would have much preferred to have been somewhere else.

Fredericka's idea of the Lady of the Manor was in the greatest conflict with the lessons she was being exposed to. Why should she be expected to learn such mundane and menial matters? Why have servants?—and she certainly intended to have servants, and plenty of them, in her household! As for being housekeeper for Uncle Janus, well, she was not about to! As long as she was here, she would go about like a good sort with the rest of her cousins since it pleased Janus, but she could never see herself as successor to her *maiden* aunt, Sophia—and she could not truly believe that anyone else could, not excluding Uncle Janus himself. She was just too beautiful a girl to have such a miserable fate meted out to her.

Jane was too fearful not to comply with her great-uncle's writ and scurried about dutifully exposing herself to the various departments of the menage. She exposed herself almost with enthusiasm but learned less than nothing from what was shown and explained to her. It was all so foreign to the way things were done at home, she discovered. Why, even the kitchen range was much too huge and its cavernous interior intimidated her. She could not begin to imagine how one was to keep track of all the linens in all the rooms, and all the laundresses that were required were enough to make her head swim. Absolutely beyond her best efforts to comprehend was the keeping of the accounts. What was the use of Addington telling her that all she need do was give her approval to his rendering of them when her head ached at the mere thought of having to be responsible for all those different sums and in such great amounts as she never had encountered in her most advanced school days. She had not been more than an indifferent scholar, and it appeared to her that she must take up all of her old lessons that she so quickly and so happily had forgotten if she were ever to take Aunt Sophia's place—not that she had the least inclination to acquire that honor. She was sure she must fail in Uncle Janus's eyes, and the thought made her very happy indeed.

Miss Harriette of the sharp tongue was, of all of the young ladies, perhaps the most agile in the mental department and, during that first week of instruction, easily absorbed all the instruction and exhibits that were presented for her edification. Coupled with her quick intelligence, there was the desire to learn, for, although she had no greater desire to play the role of Aunt Sophia to Uncle Janus than any of the other of her cousins, she did nurse an ambition of being a Lady of the Manor in her own right, and it was perfectly clear to her that when she had achieved the role of baroness, countess, or duchess even—her ambition knew no limit in that direction, even though her prospects of ever meeting a ranking peer were quite dim—having the knowledge of how to manage an establishment on the scale of Pickering Hall would be quite invaluable.

Not far behind Harriette in understanding was Phoebe. Although she made no effort to apply herself to the business at hand, it was all so simple to her comprehension that she had not the least difficulty in absorbing all the various functions and duties and offices that made up the Pickering Hall estate. As her only ambition was to be returned to the bosom of her family and take up once again the even tenor of her life in Stevenage, she showed none of the enthusiasm of Harriette. Certainly she was far above manifesting the confusion that characterized Jane's efforts, and, as it was a matter of intellectual curiosity to examine into the affairs of a great estate, she bore none of those superior airs with which Fredericka managed to try everyone's patience. As long as she was bound to stay at Pickering Hall, learning about how things were done there was something to occupy her thoughts. As to gaining the post of housekeeper to Uncle Janus, she was perfectly sure it would never come to her as she had a plan to insure it should not.

The Duke of Grade was not a religious man, and, as he had some three livings in his keeping in Cornwall, he went about in the assumption that by keeping them occupied with competent clergymen, he was doing his bit to enlighten the world and did not need to concern himself further with his own salvation. Therefore, he rarely went to church, much to the dissatisfaction of the local clergy who did not hold their livings at his pleasure.

Practicality rather than the exigencies of religion caused him to observe Sundays as days of rest, and so, upon the Sunday which succeeded the week of the young ladies familiarizing themselves with the intricacies of Pickering Hall's management, a holiday was declared, and the five grandnieces were given the day to do as they pleased. Away from the discipline of their families, they all rejected any idea of attending services at the nearby church and elected, unanimously, to ride out about the grounds and picnic as far from the Hall and Uncle Janus as they could get without leaving the bounds of his estate—which was quite far.

During the week that had passed, there had not been any great interference with the household routines, and, with them absent from the house, his Grace was very much at ease and quite satisfied that all was going well. Alas, poor man! Things were nothing like.

The girls rode out with vigour, the result of being pent up for so many days without the smallest amusement, and the sheer joy of dashing madly over the well-tended grounds gave them such a feeling of release that it was some hours before they had had enough and decided to rest next to a grove of trees, which served to tether their mounts and to cast a pleasant shade upon their picnicking.

They were all full of good spirits now and hungry and quickly settled down to the food that they had brought along with them.

While they munched upon sandwiches of cold meat slices, Fredericka took it upon herself to open the discussion of that which they were all trying so hard to put out of their minds for the day.

"Cousins, I would know who of us wishes to become housekeeper at Pickering Hall."

She was greeted with a chorus of groans.

Harriette snapped at her: "Oh, do be quiet, Fredericka! Must you spoil this one day of mild rejoicing that has been allowed us?"

"Well really, Harriette, I was only trying to come to a conclusion that might be of the greatest help to all of us."

"And what brilliant masterstroke of planning has occurred to you, may I inquire?"

"If you are going to take that tone with me, I am sure I shall not say another word!" retorted Fredericka, sulking.

"Oh, let her speak!" interjected Phoebe. "It is a topic we are all concerned with, and I venture to say that any suggestion that has the least hope in it for us is worth our giving ear to."

Philomena and Jane nodded vigorous assent, and Harriette retired, waving her hand in begrudging consent.

Fredericka cast a haughty look upon her defeated cousin and said: "Pray say which of you has a wish to remain with Uncle Janus."

There was complete silence.

"Oh, I say that is not at all fair! There has got to be at least one of us to wish it or it will never work!" she said petulantly.

"What will not work?" asked Phoebe. "If what you have in mind is so quickly defeated, it could not have been very much, I am sure."

"Well, if but one of us had the wish to be the Mistress of Pickering Hall, it would be the easiest thing for the rest of us to do all in our power to make her look the most competent in Uncle Janus's sight, don't you see?"

Harriette replied: "I am sure we see well enough, and it would not have needed a witless marvel to bring it to our attention, but in case you have not noticed, there is not a one amongst us who has a care for the honor. Now pray, inform us, my brilliant beauty, in what case that leaves us."

"Well, it is surely the simplest thing! If no one wants it, we must draw lots. It is better that one of us be sacrificed than that—"

"Why, that is the most nonsensical rubbish I ever—!" Phoebe began to protest.

"Wait, Phoebe! Let our precious cousin finish!" interrupted Harriette. "I believe we have yet to plumb the depths of Fredericka's incredible cunning."

"I was only going to add that of course you would not expect me to join in the drawing, for it is so obvious that I am eminently unfit for any such position of housekeeper—"

Harriette's mocking laughter cut her short.

Phoebe was not so amused. She retorted: "Fredericka, in the first place one of us will be *chosen*, so what advantage can there be to a drawing—"

"I was only trying—" Fredericka began defensively.

"—and in the second place none of us are *eminently* suited to being companion to Uncle Janus. I have a better idea, and it is not so wonderful. We each of us carry on as best we can and pray fervently that his Grace's blessing falls upon the others. Truly there is naught else that we can do. No matter what luck we shall have at drawing straws, Uncle Janus will not be bound by it and will make his selection as it pleases him, not us. We have had the misfortune of being born Harewoods, and this is our fate."

Harriette conferred a sharp look upon her cousin's mild features. Then she turned to the rest and declared: "Cousin Phoebe is right. I say enough of this dismal topic and let us enjoy ourselves for the moment. We are helpless in the matter, and it is purely profitless to chew upon it any further."

There was an exchange of glances and everyone appeared to agree, even Fredericka.

That evening at the dinner table, his Grace, for the first time, reintroduced the very topic that was so exercising the minds of his young guests.

At the end of the meal, he stood up and stared at each lady in turn. By the time he had made the round, their tongues were stilled, and their eyes were riveted upon him.

He gave a little nod of satisfaction and began to speak:

"Ladies of Harewood, it gives me great pleasure to extend to you my compliments upon your industry and your devotion to my wishes. I have it upon good report that each of you has done as well as might be expected in gaining a working familiarity of Pickering Hall and my particular needs. Yes, those are the very words of the commendation I received from Addington when I queried him regarding the progress you were making. Now, one may take exception to such lukewarm endorsement, but I know better. One must consider that, for all Addington knows, he may be commenting upon the efficacy of his future mistress, so, being a wise man and an even wiser butler, he refrains from overpraise lest he be overwhelmed by the gratitude of said future Mistress of Pickering Hall. You must all see at once how blessed are we at having so brave a butler in our midst.

"Nevertheless, I am sure I am quite safe in seeing the true merit of Addington's commendation that he has so well hidden with his tepid humor. I am sure it will be a most difficult choice facing me a se'nnight hence, and I promise you it will be a choice that is all fairness and justice. It shall be a choice that must reestablish Pickering Hall to the spirit instilled in it by my lamented sister, the late Lady Sophia.

"Tomorrow begins the moment when each of you, armed with all the secrets of the Hall, will venture eagerly forth and secure to yourself the management of both this, the estate of Grade and, of course, the ease and comfort of Grade. Believe me when I say that my eagerness to observe you in your new stations is a match for your own. It is, therefore, with pride and satisfaction that I bid you good night. God bless you, my dears, and God save—me!"

With that he dashed down his serviette and strode from the room, again forgetting to take up his walking stick.

Said Philomena: "I do not think his Grace is as pleased with us as he said."

"Well, that is hardly anything to upset one," remarked Harriette. "It is just possible that by the end of next week, his Grace may have found cause to reconsider his design and seek out a proper housekeeper, *I* am thinking."

"And I!" "And I!" they chorused.

Early the next morning, the young ladies were about the various allotted tasks, and the household managed to progress without a murmur—at least until breakfast was served to the duke, when his roar of complaint must have been heard quite clearly through every chamber of the great Hall.

"Addington, WHAT IS THIS?" shouted his Grace, looking with disgust down into his plate.

"Er—if it please your Grace, an omelet."

59

"An omelet—for my breakfast? Damnation, I have never eaten an omelet for breakfast in my life! Rot you, man, you know it is a coddled egg and toast for me! It has been a coddled egg and toast for me for breakfast ever since I can recall, and that was long before you ever came into my service! How dare you to disregard my pleasure? If her ladyship were only about I should have you sacked on the spot. Now take this rubbish back to the kitchen and demand a coddled egg for me! At once, do you hear? What in blazes has gotten into you, man, why do you stand about like a lump? I have given you an order, blast you!"

"Indeed, your Grace, I expressly requested your usual egg but—er—it was countermanded. I assure you, your Grace, it did me not the least good to debate the point."

"Hey? What nonsense are you talking? You are the butler, and you carry out my wishes. Sack the chef on the instant, do you hear!"

"I beg your Grace's pardon for daring to contradict, but I assure you it was not the fault of René. Indeed it was not, your Grace."

"Oh? May I be so bold as to inquire who else had the temerity to countermand my orders?" asked his Grace in the most acid tones.

"Er—as a matter of fact, your Grace, it could be that countermand is too strong a term—"

"Stop trying to split hairs with me! My breakfast egg is a standing order. I have here before me an omelet. This is countermanding my order, damn it!"

"Yes, your Grace, the fact of the matter is that the mistress—er—one of the new mistresses thought it best to serve you with an omelet."

60

"Oh, she did, did she? Which of them has the kitchen this morning?" demanded the duke.

"Miss Jane, your Grace."

"Send her to me!"

Jane, all fearful, came hesitantly into the dining room.

The duke never gave her a chance to speak, but launched into his attack at once. "So, my own ungrateful relation ventures to stab her kind old uncle in the back with an omelet. How do you dare to take such liberties with me, Miss?"

"Oh, your Grace, I—I ass-ssure y-you, it could not be helped. You s-see, this morning's eggs got broken up a bit and—and I-I thought—that is, we thought, since you must have your egg, an omelet would do?" she wound up asking a question hoping to mollify the old gentleman.

"No, it won't do! It won't do at all! I demand a coddled egg! Now see to it!"

Jane just remained standing there and began to weep.

"Oh, for God's sake, child, I am not going to eat you! Look you, I humbly beg your forgiveness for my display of temper. I assure you there is naught to be upset about. Now do be a good girl and have a coddled egg brought to me," he pleaded, carefully disguising his annoyance with carefully modulated tones.

"I ca-a-an't!" wailed Jane.

"Now why in heaven's name not?" wearily asked the duke.

"It is because all the fresh eggs were broken, your Grace."

"*All* of them? Every mother's son of them?"

61

Jane nodded and looked as though she was about to fall into tears again.

"No, I pray you will not," responded the duke, waving his hand and then placing it upon his fevered brow. "It is all right, I tell you. I will eat the omelet and without complaint, I assure you. See, I am eating it," he said with an ingratiating smile, as he lifted a portion to his lips with his fork.

He bit into it with a crunch. His mouth popped open and his fork fell clattering into the plate. Hurriedly he emptied the mouthful into his serviette and gasped: "Eggshells!"

"D-don't you like it, your Grace? Phoebe was sure you would."

His Grace stared at her in amazement, his mouth opening and closing. But words failed him, and he was reduced to shaking his head. At last he regained control of his voice and, taking a deep breath, he asked: "Phoebe thought I would like it with eggshells in it?"

"Yes, your Grace."

"She said that, did she? His Grace is fond of having eggshells in his omelet."

"Well, I do not think she was all that sure. It was her thought that with your humor, you must have a fondness for crisp foods, and she thought it would be a shame to deny you that, especially as your chef was crying and refused to take the shells out of the eggs. I did not know what else to do as your Grace had to have your egg."

"My chef was crying, you say?"

"Oh, indeed. Though I do not see why. Just because Phoebe accidentally knocked his eggs to the floor—well, really, he just stood there, the tears streaming down his cheeks, moaning: 'Tous mes oeufs jolis! Tous mes oeufs jolis!' I guess little things like that bother foreigners."

"I see. Very well, Jane, you may return to your duties—and, here, take these eggs back with you. There's a dear."

"Then your Grace did not care for the eggs that way after all?"

"No, dear, and I do apologize. I have an odd taste for having my eggshells served outside of the egg."

"Oh, I see—though I do not think that is odd at all. I prefer them that way, too," she replied, quite soberly, as she picked up his plate and withdrew from the dining room.

For a moment the duke remained staring at the door, a look of incredulity upon his face.

"God!" he muttered, and then he screamed: "ADDINGTON!"

The butler came in at once.

"You called, your Grace?"

"No, you blasted idiot, I screamed! What the devil is going on in that kitchen?"

"I hate to say, sir."

"Well, I hate to hear you say! I suppose we shall have to find us a new chef."

"It is too early to say. René has not stopped crying yet, your Grace."

"Egad, a new chef *and* a new housekeeper! Oh, this place will be in a shambles, I tell you!"

"Yes, your Grace, I fear so."

"Well, at any rate, the selection of Lady Sophia's successor has become something easier to decide. I believe we can put Miss Jane and Miss Phoebe out of consideration."

"Yes, your Grace."

"Well, don't stand there gabbing! I have lost all appetite for breakfast. Bring coffee to me in the reading room, and where is the newspaper?"

"Ah yes, your Grace. The newspaper," he said, slipping it out from under his coat and handing it to the duke.

The duke regarded him queerly. "Devil of a place to keep my newspaper, don't you think?"

"Er—there is a bit of cleaning going on about the premises, your Grace. I thought it would be safer—er—"

"Yes, yes! I see what you mean," responded his Grace testily.

He stood up from the table and prepared to withdraw.

"Er—your Grace, perhaps you would prefer tea," suggested Addington, diffidently.

"I said coffee!" replied the duke imperiously.

"Ah—um—er, your Grace—"

"Well, what is it, man? Speak up!"

"There is no coffee this morning, I regret to say. As I said, your Grace, there is a bit of cleaning going on about the premises."

"And the coffee urn is being—" added the duke nodding.

"Exactly, your Grace."

"Blast! Then make it tea!" cried the duke, and he stormed out of the room, unfolding his newspaper as he went.

"Yes, your Grace," whispered Addington, beginning to clear the table.

The Duke of Grade entered his reading room, his nose buried in his paper, went over to his favorite chair and sat himself down.

Unfortunately for his noble dignity, and even more

unfortunately for the ducal rump, there was no chair!

"Egad!" yelped his Grace, clambering to his feet, grimacing with pain as he rubbed his aching backside. "What is going *on!*"

He went over to the bellrope and gave it a furious yank. The brocaded sash heroically did its duty, but just, and then gave up its hold upon the bell lever, cascading sinuously to the floor. His Grace aimed a kick at it just as Addington came into the room.

Seeing the bellrope lying detached on the floor, he said: "I shall have it attended to at once, your Grace."

"To hell with it! What has been done with my chair?"

Addington stared helplessly at the spot that the chair had occupied down the years and scratched his head.

"I really cannot say, your Grace. I cannot imagine that it had the least need of being cleaned—"

"Oh, stop your gibbering and find it, man! Have it brought here at once!"

It must have been all of a quarter of an hour before the precious piece of furniture entered the reading room, carefully carried by two footmen. They set it down before his Grace and awaited his instructions.

His Grace squinted his eyes at it and sniffed. Muttering: "Oh no, it cannot be!" he came closer and sniffed again.

"Take it away!" he shouted. "ADDINGTON!" he screamed.

This time the butler was panting as he hurried into the room.

"Yes, your Grace!" he gasped.

"What the devil is wrong with you? You are heaving like a broken-winded nag!"

"I beg your pardon, your Grace. I see the chair has arrived—"

"It is going out! It is ruined! It smells of the stalls! Have you no nose, man? What chucklehead had it dragged out to the stables—and why?"

"Your Grace, it is a horror, indeed!" exclaimed Addington, looking as though he was about to bawl. He made a signal, and the footmen went out with it.

"I am in no need of your belated confirmation! I wish to know who perpetrated this dastardly deed?"

"I suggest you confer with the particular mistress who may be respons—"

"Find her and send her in to me! I suppose it is that silly Grantham female. Well, she shall hear it from me, I tell you!"

Addington scurried out and the duke began to pace up and down the reading room, muttering curses until the air was blue with his anger.

The door opened behind him and he wheeled, a dark scowl upon his countenance. At once the scowl was wiped away to be replaced by a charming smile as he greeted Fredericka.

"Come in, my dear. How are you this fine morning? Is everything to your taste?"

"Oh, I am quite content, Uncle Janus," she replied, smiling sweetly.

"Do sit down and tell me about it," said the duke, holding a chair for her. "I do declare that you must be the most beautiful Harewood that ever was. It does my heart proud to know that the Harewoods can claim such beauty for their own."

"Thank you, Uncle Janus. You are a very sweet gentleman, and I am so glad that you are my uncle."

"Then are we both pleased and proud. Now what can I do for you, Fredericka?"

66

"Why nothing, your Grace," she said in surprise. "Addington informed me that you had a wish to speak with me."

His Grace frowned. "No, I never—" he paused and stared at her for a moment. "Ah—did you have anything to do with the disposition of the chair that was in this room by any chance?"

"Indeed, I did!" she said proudly. "Today is my turn at overseeing that the furniture, hangings, and plate are rendered spotless."

"Oh? But my chair—it is a favorite, you know—and it needed no more than a dusting and perhaps a whisking at most."

"Oh, that is too bad, Uncle. You ought to have told me. I shall have it seen to immediately—although I am sure it will not be any the worse for its airing. Not to worry—"

"Airing? In the stables? Now, that is a mighty strange place to air anything, I am thinking."

Fredericka laughed. "Oh, how you joke, Uncle. Never *in* the stables, I assure you. Merely close by them."

"Why, in God's name, anywhere near them at all, might I ask?"

"I was told that there is always a breeze near to them, and that must make it all the better to air things. Why do you look at me that way, Uncle Janus. Is something wrong?"

The duke stared at his niece for a piece before he asked: "Did it not occur to you that close by to the stables must be a most noisome situation for such a purpose?"

"Well, of course it did!" she exclaimed laughing, "but Phoebe informed me the wind was always in the other direction and that she had heard Addington mention the fact of it having been Aunt Sophia's regular practice to have things aired out there."

"Phoebe?" asked his Grace weakly.

"Oh, yes, Uncle Janus! She is frightfully clever and so quick to learn, I am sure she would make you an excellent housekeeper."

"Thank you, Fredericka. I strongly suspect that Phoebe would be overwhelmed with pleasure to learn of your high regard for her."

"Oh, your Grace," she rushed on to say, "it is hardly worth mentioning. It is nothing."

"Yes. And thank you again, Fredericka, you have been most helpful. I give you leave to return to your duties."

Fredericka arose, performed a curtsey to her uncle, and left the room.

"ADDINGTON!"

Addington came stumbling into the room, his eyes popping with exhaustion. He was too breathless to speak.

"Ah, there you are! I smell a plot. What think you of Miss Phoebe?"

"If it please you, your Grace, the young lady is in no way exceptional."

"Oh, blast your mealy mouth! As much can be said for any of 'em!"

"Yes, your Grace."

"Don't stand there and jabber at me, man! Speak to the point! What is the girl supposed to be doing today?"

"She is out looking over the keeping of the grounds."

"Amazing!"

"I do not follow you, your Grace."

"I would think that if she is out upon the grounds,

she of any of them must be the last to have been able to interfere with my comfort; yet, by heaven, it would appear that that is actually all she seems to have devoted herself to this dreadful morning. Tell me something, Addington, you have been in an excellent position to make a determination of the qualities of these young ladies of mine. If you had to choose amongst 'em, which would you say comes closest to Lady Sophia in cleverness and humor."

"Oh, your Grace, that is never for me to say—"

"Cease your impertinence and do not talk back to me! I demand to know your opinion and do not come over me with a bunch of rubbishy tergiversations. I, Grade, demand to know."

"Yes, your Grace. If it please your Grace, I must confess that it is between Miss Phoebe and Miss Harriette. They are both of them quick and they are both of them sharp-tongued—er—that is, I mean to say, witty as was our late beloved mistress."

"Hmmm. And what of Miss Philomena?"

"A very sweet young lady, your Grace."

The duke gave him a look of impatience. "If you mean she will not do, say she will not do!"

"She will not do, your Grace."

"So it is between Miss Phoebe and Miss Harriette, is it? Well, for my money, the Grantham girl is a wonder, and, if Miss Harriette is of any greater capability, then surely all that there is left for *her* to do is to assassinate me! Well, I pray that she does whatever she is going to do soon, before that Miss Phoebe drives me out of my mind! I shudder to think that we have yet six more of such days as this to suffer through—and this one but barely begun!"

Chapter V

ALTHOUGH THINGS SETTLED down to a level of minor turbulence at Pickering Hall for the rest of that first day of trial, his Grace's humor was not any the more tranquil for it. He believed himself fly to all that was going on in his domicile and was resolved to see his purpose accomplished and the bevy of vixens he was entertaining bent to his will. The trouble was that the uncertainty of the nature of the next calamity to be foisted upon him was unnerving to a degree. He could not be sure that Phoebe had done her worst, and there was still Harriette to be heard from. He was constantly at having to stifle the strong temptation to pack them all off and hire himself a strange housekeeper. Only the fact that such servants were grown mighty independent these days and would never stand for long the truculence of his temper made him hold his peace. There was nothing like a poor relation to fill such a post.

Try as he might, his Grace could not put the menace of the young ladies out of his thoughts, and he went warily about the Hall, flinching at shadows to such an extent that by nightfall, he was truly fit to be tied.

Dinner that evening was a most uncomfortable affair. The duke did not trust himself to speak and remained toying with his food while his gaze searched the innocence in the sweet young faces of his nieces. He paid particular attention to the visages of Harriette and Phoebe, hoping to discover some clue as to the outrageous discomforts they had to be planning for his benefit. But alas! poor man that he was, he was no match for the amassed feminine guile that was seated before him at his board, and his irritation with the impossible situation gnawed away at his nerves.

None of the girls had anything at all to say, but that they were under a strain, too, was obvious. They each of them would cast a covert glance at their great-uncle occasionally and then survey their fellow cousins as though they too were searching for hints as to what was in each other's mind.

Under such conditions it can be imagined that dinner was quickly over and, with little ceremony, all retired to their bedchambers. In the duke's case, it was more a hasty retreat than a retirement.

Once within his rooms, the duke felt the tension drop away. Here, in his inner sanctum, he was safe and would continue to be safe until he had to venture forth on the morrow and face whatever it was that his loving nieces had arranged for his entertainment. Not that all worry had departed, for there was still Harriette to be heard from. He actually trembled at what must occur at her hands for he was sure that she must be a deal more cunning than all the rest. But, if Phoebe was indeed using her other cousins as her pawns, he had to admire the way she was going about it—but it puzzled him to understand her purpose. He had been sure all of them were most reluctant to have this great honor placed upon their shoulders, yet here was Phoebe going to all lengths to make her cousins look grossly incompetent while he had not heard a word reflecting upon her own competence. He shrugged his shoulders. Maybe he was in error, and there *was* a one of them eager for the post.

His valet helped him to disrobe and get in to his nightshirt. Carefully placing his night cap upon his silvery locks, hardly thinned at all by age—a fact he was quite vain of—he stepped up to his great bed and stretched and yawned. Aa-a-ah! but he was fatigued and could use a good night's rest. Quickly, he slipped between the sheets and felt his toe catch. There was a sound of ripping linen and, as nimbly he had entered the bed, so quickly did he shoot forth out of it.

Standing alongside the offending furniture with his hands upon his hips, he fumed: "So! We finally hear from Miss Harriette! What the devil is going on under the cover?" he asked himself as he took up the lamp by his bedside and threw back the covers of the bed.

Sheets, fit only for rags, greeted his eyes. Except for the spot his great toe had gone through, they were threadbarely transparent. He poked with an idle finger, and it went right through the aged and worn fabric.

He called for his valet and instructed him to rouse Addington.

In a little while, the butler appeared in a state of disarray, an expression of suffering upon his features. Dazedly, he responded to his Grace's inquiries concerning the one responsible for the state of his bedclothes and confirmed the duke's suspicion that, indeed, the linens had been the charge of Miss Harriette that day.

"I thought as much," remarked the duke, quite calmly, "and I expected as much. Very well, if I am

73

to be denied my rest, the least I can do is to grant that same favor to the culprit responsible. Send Miss Harriette to me, here!"

"Here, your Grace?" mumbled Addington. "Your bedchamber?"

"Yes, here in my bedchamber shall I interrogate her—the circumstances of her crime displayed before her very eyes! She'll not be able to deny such glaring evidence. Go fetch her!"

Addington stumbled groggily from the room.

"Young lady, I bid you regard that bed and dare to say it is a proper bed!" challenged his Grace as, garbed in a nightrobe, Harriette made her appearance.

"Oh heavens!" exclaimed Harriette. "How could that have happened? I assure your Grace that they were perfectly good sheets when I had them taken from the linens room."

"Indeed! Sheets that are so threadbare they have not the strength of cobwebs, and you tell me they were perfectly good sheets to begin with. My, how thoroughly they have worn themselves out in a matter of hours!"

Harriette looked all confusion as she protested: "Oh, I did not think that they were all that worn. I thought that surely they were the finest sheets that ever I had seen and that nothing less was appropriate for the bed of so great and wealthy a nobleman such as you, your Grace."

The duke nodded with satisfaction. "Yes, and I dare say you had that brilliant inspiration from Cousin Phoebe, I do not doubt."

Harriette frowned in indignation. "That is not true, your Grace! I thought it all out myself—"

She stopped herself in midsentence, clapping a hand over her mouth, a look of panic in her eyes.

The duke threw up his hands and turned his back upon her. "You are excused, Harriette. Go back to bed. I shall have something to say to all of you in the morning. Good night."

Harriette, red-faced with embarrassment, scurried out.

The duke turned about, and there was a triumphant grin upon his face.

Murmuring to himself, he said: "I venture to say the siege is over. I have got me my mistress of the manor. Now I can get some rest. It has been a hard and longish day."

Bundling up the collection of tatters from the bed, he stepped over to an adjoining chamber and hammered on the door.

His valet stuck a sleepy head out, and his Grace thrust the demolished bed linen at him.

"Give me your sheets, man, and take these rags for yourself until morning. I'll be doubledamned if I am going to rouse the household over such a measly business of fresh sheets!"

Chapter VI

THE NEXT MORNING, the five cousins were scattered about the house taking their turns at ordering a different portion of the Hall's domestic economy. Phoebe found herself in the kitchen consulting with René on the menu for the day. The chef was rattling off a list of dishes dear to his heart which, Phoebe suspected, would do little good to her uncle's ancient stomach. No doubt René was taking the opportunity to prepare *specialités* from the French cuisine that were all but mere memories to him, and he was not only supplying the names of these labors of the heart, but insisted on going off into gastronomic rhapsodies on their flavorings and textures, all in French, of course. Phoebe was able to follow him pretty well, but it was a bit of a bother because her mind was concerned with more momentous thoughts. In any event she did not care what René wished to prepare, believing that she would not remain under the duke's roof much longer. She was so sure that her plan would work out and set her free of the place.

She giggled with delight when Addington came down to the kitchen to inform her that his Grace required her presence in the reading room. Since the butler appeared to be very stiff about it, she was sure it was a sign that what she had been at such pains to achieve the day before had already born fruit, and, head on high, she followed Addington out, bracing herself for the storm of the old man's fury.

Addington knocked respectfully at the door of the reading room, and his Grace snarled a "Come!" from within.

The butler swung the door open, and Phoebe marched in, proudly erect, even though her stomach was churning with anxiety over the awful encounter about to commence.

"Ah, Phoebe, my dear, do come in and find yourself a chair," he said cordially.

Addington was about to retire, but the duke snapped: "No, not yet, Addington! There is some business for you to observe. You will kindly pay your respects to Miss Phoebe, Mistress of Pickering Hall," he announced.

Addington let out a sigh and bowed to Phoebe. "It will be my pleasure to serve you, Mistress."

"Excellent, Addington! Now go and inform your subordinates and colleagues of the news. Pickering Hall has found its Mistress."

"Very good, your Grace." He bowed to the duke and then bowed to Phoebe. "Miss Phoebe," he said and withdrew.

Phoebe was in a state of shock. She could not believe it was happening to her—the very fate she had labored so industriously to avoid! She sat numbly, looking askance at her great-uncle. Could the old man be so far gone as to have grown senile? she wondered. Oh, but no! He was a most alert old gentleman and shrewd even as he sat and stared back at her, the slightest sneer upon his lips.

No, his Grace had made a horrible mistake! It was

78

one of the others that he had meant this honor for—and, quickly, she must show him the error in his judgement.

Summoning up all her courage, she said: "Your Grace does me far too much honor. In fact, I believe it an honor intended for one of my cousins. If your Grace will be kind enough to inform me of whom it is, I shall be glad to fetch her," and she stood up.

"Sit down, young lady! There is no mistake, and all of my faculties are A1, so do not try to come a Miss Saucebox over me. You are, as of here and now, my Mistress of Pickering Hall. With my own hand I have elected you to that high office, and I expect you will serve me, Grade, with all due respect and courtesy making every provision for my comfort and the smart running of my establishment. To you will be accorded all high honor and distinction and, by my soul, you are now of right the first lady of the Harewoods! *That* is no *little* distinction—nor are all the comforts and luxuries you are surrounded by, and are now the mistress of, to be taken lightly. I would hear your words of appreciation of this mark of my favor."

Phoebe arose from her chair and sank into a deep curtsey to his Grace. Rising, she addressed him:

"Your Grace, you may believe that I am overwhelmed at the compliment you intend, but, in truth, it is not one I sought nor merited. I, who have never wished for aught but the bosom of my family, certainly I am ill-prepared to support the manner of so grand an establishment as Pickering Hall. Now that I have enjoyed the privilege of examining into all the intricacies of this noble establishment, I am filled with the awe of great respect for Aunt Sophia and am well aware that I could never measure up to her high standards. I never can, nor do I have any wish to even try, your Grace. Truly, I am ill-suited for this responsibility and undeserving of this high recognition."

His Grace clapped his hands vigorously in applause.

"Dear Phoebe, that has got to be the most exquisite performance it has been my good fortune to witness. You give an old man great pleasure and whet my appetite for many future such diversions!"

Phoebe frowned in annoyance. "Your Grace, I would point out to you that I am all seriousness and never intended to amuse you."

"Nevertheless, you have, my dear, and I am pleased to have you with me."

"But I have no wish to stay with you! I can never cope with it all, nor am I one for all this dignified station and duty. I have had no experience—"

"Bah! You talk like a child! Your Aunt Sophia had even less experience—as though any noble woman worth her salt needs experience! It is in your blood, girl! And do not speak of this nonsense of merit and reward. Of couse you have not *earned* it, so, just between us, it is no reward at all. But do not think for one moment that I have been arbitrary in my choice, young lady, for I most certainly have not. I chose you because you are the best of the lot—and not a very good lot it was, I do not mind telling you! Every last one of you ungrateful girls returned the honor and the hospitality I accorded you with schemes and plots to defeat me in my purpose. Well, know you that you only defeated yourself! I was on to your little scheme quite early in the game. You shall have to get up a deal earlier than that before you can hope to fool your Uncle Janus, by God!"

Phoebe stood before him, a most puzzled look upon

her face. She put out her hands in a gesture of bewilderment.

"Do you tell me, your Grace, that—"

" 'Uncle' will do nicely. As you are now a member of my particular family, I see no need for any excessive formality between us, Phoebe."

"Thank you, Uncle Janus, but what I mean to say is, why must you single me out for punishment? My other cousins had no better attitude towards this distinction you insist on forcing upon me than I—and it appeared to me that they have behaved far worse than I in the performance of their duties."

The duke chuckled and raised his eyes in appreciation. "Oh, you are a one!" he cried, raising an admonishing finger at her. "How quickly you can steer with the wind! Indeed I am all admiration, Phoebe. You are trying to have it both ways now, are you not?"

"I am sure I do not know what you mean, Uncle Janus."

"Oh, do sit down, for heaven's sake! This is not a royal audience!"

Never taking her eyes off him, Phoebe slowly subsided into her chair.

"Young lady, you have shown me your mettle and now you are challenging me!" he said forcefully.

Phoebe started to object, but he waved her to be silent. "No, no, let me speak, for, if we are to get along together—and I am determined that we shall—I have got to show you my mettle so that you will know exactly with whom you have to deal.

"It began with my breakfast egg—a most skillful ploy on your part, I must say, for it had me quite convinced that neither you nor Jane would suit—and, if it had stopped there, I suppose I should be speaking with Harriette at this moment instead of you. But, when horror after horror was perpetrated upon my poor household by one and all of my devoted nieces, and always was Phoebe's name connected with each and every one of them—save one—it was obvious to me that here was a girl of extravagant cunning and of a brilliance of mind that must gain from me, certainly, my profound respect. I bid you examine the events as I have done. There was planning—and on the very shortest notice. There was execution—and of such a subtlety that your pawns of cousins never suspected what you were up to. And last but not least was your estimate of my reactions and of my habits. You planned it that I should become aware of all that you were doing to my discomfitting. Ah, but my dear, you planned too well! Can you not see now that all these qualities you were displaying—all of these very qualities—were exactly what I should require in the Mistress of Pickering Hall? Yes, my dear, although you bear no resemblance to your Aunt Sophia, yet could you have been her daughter. I am perfectly satisfied that I could not have found a better young lady-relation for my purpose."

Phoebe was blushing. She felt as though her innermost thinking had been rudely put on display and experienced a sinking feeling that she was no match for her Uncle Janus. The thought filled her with a great respect for him, but did nothing to augment her liking for her august relative, nor did it completely discourage her from playing her last card.

She said: "Uncle Janus, I am embarrassed that you have found me out so easily. But I—"

"I say! You do yourself too little credit, my dear—and me, too! I venture to say it was very well done of you. Addington had not the slightest notion of what you were up to, and there never can be the least doubt but that your cousins were in the same case with him. As for myself, I had rejected you at your first effort, and, indeed, it was a masterstroke. Eggshells in my omelet!" He chuckled. "Oh, and the implied insult! His Grace must prefer crisp foods to go with his crisp humor!" He laughed. "Oh, that was very good, my dear, and you had such a perfect foil in Jane. Yes, had you left the business at that point, I should never have given you another thought. When I had put it all together, I had only the deepest admiration for you. I dare say Harriette was too sharp for you to have made use of her, but she was never so sharp as you. Yes, my dear Phoebe, grandniece and great-uncle, we are a well matched pair, indeed, I expect we shall get on very well together."

"But, Uncle Janus, you can no longer be in any doubt of my dislike for the honor. That in itself must speak to the dismal prospect that must be in store for both you and me. I should ever resent the fate that binds me to Pickering Hall."

"Bah! That is childish nonsense and you will soon get over it!" he retorted testily.

"Show me a slave that loves his chains," Phoebe said sulkily.

His Grace sat up straight in his chair and glared at her. "Now that, young lady, will be about enough from you! I shall not tolerate pure impertinence! Look about you! All is at your command and at your pleasure! Slave, indeed! I can show you myriads of freemen who would gladly accept chains for but a taste of it! You are speaking nonsense!"

Phoebe was breathing heavily, and she glared right back at her uncle.

"Your Grace, it comes down to this. You shall have

83

to force me to stay. If you do, then truly I am not free!"

His Grace was quite angry now. He raised his hand and shook a menacing finger at her.

"You are free to do as you like! This is England, and no Harewood was ever slave to any man! You prattle on about slavery as though you know what it was. Believe me you do not, if you can equate that abomination with the honor I am trying to bestow upon you. That is the trouble with you young people; you deal with your notions as though they were realities. Indeed, Miss, you have a great deal to learn, and you had better start in at once.

"Here is reality. I am Grade and I am a Harewood, *the* Harewood, and wealthy beyond your most extravagant dreams. You are a Harewood, and, like all the rest of the Harewoods, the only asset you can boast of is your tie of blood to Grade. You have nothing else. Your parents have nothing else. Without my favor, there is not one amongst you who could make a better appearance before the world than a mere yeoman's family. Think upon that, Miss Phoebe Grantham, and think carefully. You are a poor relation as are all the Harewoods, and know that being a poor relation is something better than being no relation to wealth at all."

Phoebe looked stricken. "D-do y-you mean to tell me that my papa depends upon your bounty for his independence?"

"I have said as much. What do you think that independence will be worth after his beloved daughter has denied her kind, generous, and affectionate uncle the sole support of her poor parents, eh? Tell me, what do I owe to you? To them, after you have rejected the honor of becoming the Mistress of Pickering Hall?"

Phoebe was quite pale. It was all up with her. There was no escape. Uncle Janus was a monster and had woven a net about her that she could never in all good conscience even try to unravel. It was all so unjust. Why could it not have been Philomena or Harriette? Why did it have to be herself that was so thoroughly trapped by the old man's cunning?

"It is not fair of you!" she protested.

He shrugged, eyeing her intently. "What has fairness got to say to the business? What is fair about anything in life, my dear? One never stops to think about one's station in life, but I bid you think on it a moment. What is so fair that I, a Harewood, should be inordinately wealthy, while all the other Harewoods are indigent? What is fair about one man being a monarch, while another man can never rise above the station of a menial?"

Phoebe was shocked. "Why—why that is blasphemy and—and treason! It is God's will!"

Uncle Janus's eyebrows lifted. "Then you, my dear, are at least as blasphemous as I am, for you are saying that God is unfair. Perhaps He is. Perhaps, if we understood what He was about, we could then see the justice in His work—but there you have it! The situation is thus and so, and you had best accept it and make the best of it. You are my Mistress of Pickering Hall, whether you think it fair or not."

Phoebe regarded her uncle for a moment, her lips trembling with the force of her emotions.

At once, Uncle Janus raised both hands in horror. "No, my dear, no tears! If I have so misjudged you only to discover that, despite those sterling qualities I prize in you, you are naught but a weepy, wailing female, you may join your cousins at once and are free to leave. That, I cannot abide!"

The temptation to do just that was strong within her, but Phoebe knew that it was not a thing she could do without feeling ashamed. Her uncle's very frankness, his willingness to concede defeat in the face of victory affected her to the point that, with sober features, she merely nodded at him and said: "Very well, Uncle Janus, you leave me no choice; yet I shall hope forever that you will retract this demand you make upon me."

"Do that, my dear, and, if it will help, but consider that nothing lasts forever, not even the seventh Duke of Grade. Now then, do you take up your responsibilities to our guests and send them packing. I, for one, have had enough of Harewood nieces to last a lifetime."

"Me?" asked Phoebe in surprise. "You wish me to send them off?"

"Naturally. You are their hostess in my name, and that is one of the more bothersome functions for which I require a Mistress of the Manor, don't you see?"

"But, Uncle Janus, I cannot just shoo them out the door and on such short notice. Their parents can never—"

"Oh, pshaw! The stables are full of carriages, and there are coachmen and footmen in excess to see them safely returned to their homes. It is all at your disposal, my dear. Now do not bother me further, and see to it."

As she arose from her chair and stood uncertainly before him, he winked at her and said: "No trouble. Just you keep Addington by your side. You will find he is a jewel."

"Thank you, Uncle Janus."

She turned and walked out of the room, forehead corrugated in thought.

The old duke watched her leave. When she was gone, he nodded his head in satisfaction and grinned. "Aye, and I venture to say that I have got me a jewel, too!"

Chapter VII

PHOEBE, her head bent in thought, walked slowly down the hall to the music room. It was an unconscious choice, yet it demonstrated her reluctance to receive her cousins in any but an informal atmosphere. She came into the room and went over to the bellrope where she paused.

She lifted her eyes to it, but she did not see it. She was thinking of how she was to conduct herself at this, the first performance of her duty as Mistress of Pickering Hall. It was no manner of use to continue in her assault upon the dignity and comfort of Uncle Janus. For one thing, he would see right through any such attempt at the outset. For another, it could only appear to him as a childish effort at revenge, and that must embarrass her. For his part, there was nothing malicious or vindictive in his selection of her for the post. Truly, to him, it was an honor he was bestowing, and she could hardly hold that against him. That he could become a menacing figure if she dared to cross him in this, she had no doubt, nor did she have any wish to embroil herself in such a hopeless struggle. She had done her best to dissuade his Grace, and he, in turn, had demonstrated his intention not to be persuaded by her. More than that she could not do, and she must resign herself to her fate—no, not resign herself! That were foolish indeed! What she had got to do was to make the best of it, do her utmost to get along with her uncle—or neither of them would be very happy.

She would continue to hope that somehow, someday, she would escape from his grasp, but, until that day dawned, she would be in fact, and in all particulars, a very Mistress of Pickering Hall. Uncle Janus would have no complaint to make of her upon that score.

She raised her hand and tugged at the bellrope. It was time to begin. She went to stand by the fireplace and waited there, silent and erect.

The door opened and Addington entered.

"You rang, Miss Phoebe?"

"Addington, I pray you will seek out my relations and bid them attend their hostess here in the music room. After you have done that, arrange for their transportation home. Three carriages with a footman and driver for each should be sufficient, don't you think?"

"Very good, Miss Phoebe, I shall see that all is in readiness."

He regarded her for a moment and then asked: "If it be your pleasure, I shall instruct the maids to begin to pack."

"Thank you, Addington. That is most thoughtful in you."

"Miss Phoebe, at his Grace's instruction you have been installed in the chambers that served Lady Sophia. I hope you will be pleased."

She nodded. "And Buckle is to continue to serve me. Do you have any objection to her being raised to that post?"

Addington looked startled. "Do you ask me, Miss Phoebe?"

"Are you not the ranking household servant? I should think your opinion invaluable in this matter."

Addington smiled. "I thank you, Miss Phoebe, and am honored by your good opinion of me. I am sure that Buckle will serve you well."

"Thank you, Addington. You may go about your tasks now."

"Thank you, Miss Phoebe," he replied. He bowed respectfully and departed.

Now Phoebe braced herself against the appearance of her cousins. It was bound to be an ordeal. She could just picture the pity in their faces and the exultation in their hearts that she and none of them had been trapped into the station not a one of them had desired.

It was a little time before all the cousins could be collected, and, as they came in, Phoebe quietly asked them to be seated until all were present. She saw the wondering looks they cast upon her. There was great curiosity and, although she could not understand it, an admixture of awe in her cousins' eyes. Surely, she wondered, they cannot envy me?

Even Fredericka appeared somewhat subdued, Phoebe marveled, and a feeling of confidence began to brew inside of her. She was the Mistress of Pickering Hall, grandniece and hostess to his Grace, Janus, Duke of Grade. Now, truly, that did have a ring of importance to it, she thought. And, too, there was a certain satisfaction to be gleaned from the fact. Was she not now something more than merely her father's daughter? Indeed she was, and her cousins were aware of it, too. Even envied her her new station.

Had they had it to do all over again, would they have been so reckless of their prospects again? Phoebe's eyebrow lifted. Gladly would she have granted them a second chance at the honor. For all the trappings and exalted family position, she wanted none of it. To go down the years tied to an ancient relative who, in a matter of a few years, must decline into valetudinarianism was not her idea of a life for a young lady. Oh, how she would miss the parties, the dances, the chances for romance! It was all just beginning for her back in Stevenage. It was not an easy thing to have to give up, not even in exchange for the sumptuous style of living she was now embarking on. Uncle Janus was never known to have given a ball or even a rout at Pickering Hall. After all, Aunt Sophia would never have required such entertainments, she was too old. As for Uncle Janus, well of course he was even older. But—she had got to put a good face upon it before her cousins. Later up in her room—Aunt Sophia's room—she could shed her tears.

Fredericka, the last to come in, took her seat and gazed at Phoebe, her beautiful blue eyes opened a little wider than usual.

Phoebe stepped forward and addressed the group of four young ladies.

"My Cousins, I have brought you together to bid you fond farewell. As you no doubt have been informed, Uncle Janus has selected a new Mistress of the Manor, myself, and it is now become my duty to see you off. Philomena, dear Cousin, favor me by stopping off at my home and informing my parents of this honor that has come to their daughter. I will prepare a letter for you to carry to them."

"Oh, yes, Cousin Phoebe, you may ask anything of

92

me," replied Philomena mournfully. Then she rose from her seat and cast herself into Phoebe's arms. "Oh, how I shall miss you back in Stevenage!" she cried tearfully.

Phoebe, feeling years older, patted her comfortingly upon the shoulder. "There, there, Philomena, I am sure that the occasion will arise when we shall visit with each other again. I am not gone from you forever. It is only a matter of forty miles, you know."

Philomena stepped back from her and asked: "But will his Grace ever allow it? Will he let you leave here?"

Thump! went a cane upon the floor and the duke was standing before them, all indignation.

"Of course, he will!" he shouted. "Rot my liver but you are, without doubt, as fearful a pack of biddies it has ever been my misfortune to entertain! Don't you dare libel me any more than you have already! Know you that your cousin Phoebe is her own mistress! She comes and goes as she likes, but Pickering Hall is now her home and her responsibility—and to her belong all the rights and privileges that accrue to the lady of this house!" and he banged his stick down upon the floor to seal his declaration. Smartly swinging it up to his shoulder, he marched out, calling: "I wish you ladies a pleasant journey home! My regards to your families."

There was not much left to be said after that, and, amidst a great deal of confusion and packing, four hours later saw the last of the Harewood grandnieces go off down the broad drive and out of Phoebe's sight.

Phoebe, feeling quite sad, stood in the doorway of the Hall, her eyes beginning to mist up.

"What is for dinner, Mistress?" asked the Duke from behind her.

She turned and dashed a tear from her eye. "Why, there is—Oh, heavens, René must not—Your pardon, your Grace, I have to attend to matters in the kitchen—At once!" she cried and fled below stairs.

The duke chuckled. "It would appear I have nipped the last of her little plots in the bud—at least I sincerely hope it is the last!"

Chapter VIII

PHOEBE WENT RACING down to the kitchen and was about to dash through its doors when she bethought herself how very unladylike she would appear, before the eyes of the help, to come into the great chamber panting like a schoolgirl after a sweet biscuit. She paused, with her hand on the latch, just long enough to catch her breath and pat her hair into place. Straightening up her shoulders, she let her expression relax into one of calm dignity and went on into the kitchen.

René's huge bulk was hovering over the range. With a large soup spoon, he was ladling up a taste from one of the many pots busily steaming and filling the air with mouth-watering aromas.

"René, we must have a different bill of fare for tonight," she said.

Slowly he revolved, the soup spoon inches from his protruding lips. Although it did not get close enough to touch them, his lips made smacking noises as he glared at Phoebe with one eye.

"Non!" he shouted, shaking his head so vigorously as to set his jowls aquiver and spill the contents of the spoon onto the floor. He never noticed and plunged the utensil into his mouth.

He plucked it forth and stared at it as Phoebe declared: "René, the menu we planned this morning is too rich for his Grace's digestion. You must prepare something of a milder sort for him."

The spoon was become an offense in his eyes, and he cast it from him. It fell clattering to the floor.

"Non! non!" he shouted. "I have created a masterpiece of a sauce! I shall call it sauce a la René! His Grace must taste of it and pay homage to the so great chef that I am! Never have I done such a wonder before! All I have cooked in this house is milk, milk, milk!"

Phoebe stood her ground firmly. "You may put a dab of your sauce on the bit of sole you will prepare for his Grace's supper—but just a dab so he may judge a taste of it."

"And fish! Fish! Fish! Non, René is *fatigué*! You broke my eggs! You would deprive me of my art! For you I have the sack!" He began stripping off his great apron.

"René, you are behaving like a child! And anyway, you cannot sack yourself! You have to be sacked by someone else! *I* certainly shall not give you the sack."

He had slipped out of the apron only to discover that he had no shirt on under it, and his great hairy chest was exposed to view. In a mass of confusion, he muttered: "*Pardon*, Ma'mselle!" and clutched the apron top to his bosom.

He looked at her and shook his head: "But of course I do not take the sack from so *petite fille* as you! I go to Monseigneur le Duc! Only so great a man as he can give the sack to René Bonlichard!"

Phoebe was studying him, her lips firmly compressed. "Very well, go to the duke. Then you may pack your things and leave. I shall prepare the sole for the duke's supper tonight."

"*Sacrebleu!* Nevair in my kitchen! Nevair do I permit—"

"But it is no longer your kitchen, René, and someone has to prepare dinner for his Grace."

"I, René, shall prepare the sole for Monseigneur le Duc, and after I give to him the sack."

Phoebe smiled with relief. How awful, if, upon her very first day in charge, she was to lose his Grace's chef.

She said: "Very well, René. I am sure that after one of your wonderful meals, his Grace will be only too happy to oblige you."

René stared at her blankly. Then he turned to stare at the collection of pots and pans on the range. "Nevair you mind, *mon petit chou-chous*, I eat you myself." Considering his girth, there could never be any doubt but that he meant what he said.

"I should be exceedingly pleased, René, if you would honor me with a taste of your masterpiece at dinner—"

Delight lit up the chef's eyes. "Oh, *mais oui,* Ma'mselle! You do me the great honor! For you, I shall prepare *un bon repas* such as nevair has been seen in thees Hall! The sole shall be excellent but for you, the young *maîtresse*, the sauce shall be a feast for a gourmet! I bid you now to taste!"

He waddled away for another spoon and was quickly at his pots, deftly dipping the utensil in and carefully lifting it out. He gave it a slight wave of the hand to cool it and proffered it to her. Suspecting that a refusal must initiate another sacking debate, Phoebe gingerly bent to the spoon and took a sip.

Indeed, it was a most delicious sauce, she thought, and did not hesitate to compliment René on his superb artistry.

René positively glowed, and the entire kitchen seemed to respond to his gladsome change of mood as he turned to his assistants, bursting with all manner of commands, heavily laced with Gallic epithets.

Phoebe, breathing a sigh of relief, slipped away to compliment herself upon her ability to cope with the temperamental Frenchman. She felt as though she had accomplished a great thing.

In the days that passed, Phoebe made the discovery that the management of the Pickering Hall menage called for a deal more than a knowledge of where the napery was kept or how many old cronies his Grace was expecting in the next few days. These were easy things to arrange and remember as compared to having to be able to strike precisely the right note when dealing with the various servants.

The temperamental talent of a René made a far greater demand upon her ingenuity than the competent composure of an Addington. And in an utterly different direction, and far more pleasant than either to meet with, was the respectful jollity to be found in the paddock and stables. Perhaps it was her love of horses and her enthusiasm for the excellent stock that his Grace kept there that eased the barriers between herself and the grooms and coachmen.

With the females of the household, it was a different story entirely. Almost instinctively, Phoebe understood that towards them she must ever be the complete lady or they would forget their place in an instant, especially those younger females who were inclined to be cheeky about everything on general principles. She thanked her lucky stars that she had decided upon Buckle for her personal maid, for that roly-poly, beaming creature had a steady head upon her shoulders, and Phoebe could say the most outrageous things to her without Buckle taking any airs upon herself that she was in her mistress's confidence.

Handling the servants so that they did their work in a more or less contented fashion was no little task, and Phoebe found that much more of her time was taken up in settling squabbles over prerogatives than in administering the Hall's affairs. But the greatest burden that fell upon her young shoulders was that of managing the humor of his Grace. He was never satisfied that anything was being done as it should and managed to fill the air at the dinner table with complaints and lamentations for the good old days when servants not only did their work without being told but were jolly well content with their lot into the bargain. If he had his way, he'd fire the lot—which was a strange thing for him to remark as he seemed to be forever getting his way. No servant was secure when his Grace came upon the scene, and Phoebe was hard put to keep all the servants he did sack out of his sight in the hope that he would forget whatever incident it was that had given him cause for dissatisfaction—and that seemed to work out well enough. If it had not, Phoebe was sure that there would not have been a member of the original staff left about the place at the end of two weeks.

Actually, the post she had taken up would have been nothing but a sinecure except for his Grace, and, as one day suceeded the next, each with at least one sacking to its credit, her feeling of being able to cope with the situation became more and more strained until she was sure that the duke must explode one day and send everyone packing. After such a cataclysmic event, it would have been impossible to have ignored the consequences, and she could contemplate what must then ensue—Pickering Hall without a servant to call its own—with utter horror.

The thought had its effect upon her own good humor, and, little by little, the strain began to tell. She became, day by day, a bit more irritable, a bit more short in her dealings with everyone, coming to resent in the extreme any of these petty businesses that were beginning to exhaust both her temper and her patience.

One day she could not stand it any more and went storming into the gun room to speak her mind to his Grace.

"Uncle Janus, it is too much! I will not have it, I tell you!"

He had a fowling piece in his hands and was looking it over. He looked over his shoulder at her and said icily: "Miss, you forget your place. *I* will not have insolence from you, do you hear?"

"Then I shall give you your choice, your Grace. You may have my insolence or you may have my absence. Enough is enough! I am doing my best to maintain the Hall and its people, and all you do is to go about forever criticizing my best efforts—and, as if that was not bad enough, today you have gone and fired two of your very best servants—"

"And good riddance, I say. Addington has been with me for so long, he goes about in the belief that he is running the place. He is grown too high-nosed for my stomach. Send off to London and procure a fellow with better sense than to pit his judgement against mine and who is not insolent into the bargain—Now, do you leave me for I am busy."

He turned his attention back to his gun, leaving her fuming at his offhanded manner.

"What do I know of butlers, your Grace! I have never engaged a single solitary servant in my life!"

He carefully placed the gun down upon the table and turned to her. She could see that he was angry.

"That is a lie, Miss! I have discharged any number of servants since you have been with me, and all you have got to do is to look about you to see that we are in no way suffering from a dearth of staff."

"Well, that, your Grace, is purely because I did not see that they should suffer because for a moment you were in your usual vile humor!" Phoebe retorted.

"You have your nerve, young lady!" he thundered.

"And you, sir, have yours! How dared you to discharge *my* personal maid. She is *my* concern and none of *yours*!"

"I'll have you know that I am the master in my house, and when I give an order to a servant, they obey it or suffer the consequences! That female had the nerve to say to me, Grade, that, as she was on her mistress's business, she would go to find someone else to assist me. I fired her on the spot!"

"Well, I rehired her on the spot! I reengaged her just as I have all the other poor souls you have tyrannized over, and Addington as well! I could never let Addington go. Who would help me to hire new domestics if not he?—"

"That makes no sense at all! What need have you of Addington to hire new when we never succeed in getting rid of the old?"

"Addington stays. He knows the Hall better than anyone, and I need him," she asserted doggedly.

The duke regarded his niece for a moment, and finally he nodded.

"Very well, he may stay on, but only at my

pleasure, you understand. The other one, the female, goes."

"No!"

"I have spoken, Miss!" he proclaimed, his eyes smoldering.

But Phoebe would not give in to him. She dipped in a respectful curtsey and said in mock humility, "In that case, your Grace, I will go with her."

The duke's eyes popped open wide and he exclaimed: "The devil you say! You will leave me when I say you shall and not a moment before!"

"No, your Grace, that is not at all correct. I may leave you at any time I choose to do so—at the risk of your displeasure, true enough, but as you have made me the Mistress of Pickering Hall, then, by God, I shall be Mistress of Pickering Hall! You may be the master here, your Grace, but as I am the mistress, you have got to leave the management to me. Whatever you may believe, I am not your puppet, and, if I consider your displeasure less than my right and privilege granted to me by your own hand, then, whatever consequences you will visit upon my family, you shall not have the satisfaction of being able to claim you bent me to your will!"

He blinked. She was standing before him erect and unyielding, even though her shoulders trembled and she had to grip her hands together to keep them from shaking.

In a milder tone, he queried: "Do you mean to say that I, Grade, under my own roof, have got to take orders and instruction from a mere snip of a girl?"

"No, your Grace, hardly that. I ask only that you let me be free to carry on with my duties without any interference. If you have any complaint to make, I pray you will make it to me. It will be my pleasure to

102

see it remedied. I certainly do not intend to see myself stripped of my help for such petty reasons as you are ever at pains to discover—"

"Petty reasons! My dear Phoebe—"

"No, your Grace, discharging one domestic after another is not any way to go about it. None of them will serve you well in such case. Why should they even try if they will only find themselves out in the cold tomorrow?"

"But surely I may give orders to my own servants?"

"Well, of course, Uncle Janus, but for heaven's sake, we have plenty about that you do not have to insist upon one who is already occupied—and my maid has got to be my maid. For as long as she is my maid, my wishes must take precedence with her—that is only natural!"

"That is only unnatural! Your Aunt Sophia never—"

"I am not Aunt Sophia! She had her way and I have mine. You chose me. If you believe you have made an error in your choice, then I suggest you give me the sack with all the rest!"

He glared at her. "By God, just to teach you a lesson, I should—but, dammit all, where shall I find another like you? Certainly not amongst the other Harewoods, I'll be bound. Young lady, I'll have you know that no one has ever dared to issue an ultimatum to Grade until now. Blast me if I like it one bit—but a good lady of the household is not easy to come by, so I shall overlook your impudence, your insolence, and your impertinence this once. But, mind you, this is my house, and, damme, I'll complain as much as I like and for as long as I like! Now get you back to your concerns and cease to bother me with your petty silliness!"

She seemed to be frozen to the spot, so he scowled at her.

She fled.

Alas! the Duke of Grade did not change his manner or his humor with the help. He was too old to change. He went about in his usual way, complaining and carping over every little thing, never saying "thank you," never commenting "well done," and, as ever before, each day witnessed another discharge or two. Still, the makeup of the domestic staff never changed. All the old faces remained at their posts. In fact, the frequency of discharges actually increased. Although Buckle was never subjected further to such disgrace, there were days when poor Addington could do nothing to the old man's satisfaction, and on such dismal days, he got the sack as many as half a dozen times.

It all went to create a much pleasanter mood about the place. It even became a bit of a game, the domestics holding lotteries as to who would be the most thoroughly sacked by the quarter's end. Of course, anyone caught cheating—that is, inviting such castigation by the truly incompetent performance of his or her duty—risked being thrown out of the game permanently—by the Mistress of the Manor.

There was no cheating.

Chapter IX

ALTHOUGH A SORT of peace had descended upon Pickering Hall, no such peace had taken hold of Phoebe's thoughts. She did not like Uncle Janus any the better for having gotten her way with him, and she was as discontented as ever with her lot. She longed to return to Stevenage, to resume the simple life she had been leading. Whatever fascination the running of a great household could have held for her, it could never compare to being with her mother at home and enjoying the socialities of the younger people of the neighborhood.

The life at Pickering Hall was no life for a young maiden at an age for romance, her head filled with dreams of beaux and weddings. Constantly haunted by the knowlege that Aunt Sophia had remained a maiden lady, it was understandable that Phoebe was not able to resign herself to a similar and lamentable fate.

It was some months later, after she had reached a state of such competence in her new station that any extraordinary demands upon her ingenuity were become few and far between, that the entire business began to pall, and she consulted with Addington about the possibility of opening the Hall to their neighbors of Richmond Hill.

"Addington, his Grace is forever closeted with his cronies, all of them gentlemen of an age with him. One would think that a glimpse of youth and the ring of gaiety and frolic in these vast chambers would be something more refreshing than his going on from day to day with never a change. I was thinking of suggesting to his Grace a party or two to relieve the dullness of existence at Pickering Hall."

"Indeed, Miss Phoebe, I am sure that such a prospect would be most welcome to all who reside within these walls. If I might speak for myself, truly, so much that I do and so much that I assign the others to do is actually to no purpose. To what avail do we polish silver that tarnishes itself without the least use? Why polish the plate that no one ever sees? The old gentlemen who call upon his Grace have no eyes for anything but the contents of the gun room, and, at times, I am come to think that the walls of the Hall itself must come crashing down with utter boredom. I am a butler and proud of my competence. It has been so long since I have enjoyed the opportunity of mounting family entertainments and formal dinners. I beg leave to say that Pickering Hall is out to pasture, as am I, as are we all. It is such a grand waste to my thinking. But, alas, what is to be done? It is long years since Lady Sophia of blessed memory dared to suggest anything of the sort to his Grace."

"What was the outcome?"

Addington shook his head sadly. "It was no manner of use. His Grace was adamant. He saw no need for any such extravagance and threatened to close the Hall and pack us all off to Cornwall. He vowed that the peace and tranquility of Pickering Hall was a thing of rare beauty and swore it should never be disturbed. Her ladyship attempted to remonstrate with him, and he shouted her down. She did not see fit to ever return to the topic again," he ended sadly.

Phoebe compressed her lips and a look of determination came into her eyes. "How long ago was this, Addington?"

The butler's forehead wrinkled in thought. "Oh, it was such a very long time ago. A dozen years perhaps, Miss Phoebe."

"Well, that has got to change. Do you give some thought to what we might undertake in the way of a suitable diversion for our friends and neighbors whilst I go to speak with his Grace."

"Miss Phoebe, I wish you all success with his Grace, but I entertain no false hopes that you will succeed with him."

But Phoebe was not to be daunted. The prospect of unending days devoted to the echoing chambers and the unvarying routines of housekeeping was not her idea of a way to go on. She was bound to see a change in them.

When she found her uncle, he was standing out upon the great lawn with his back to the Hall, leaning upon his cane. He appeared to be surveying the scene, casting an occasional look into the distance where the buildings of London, dwarfed to insignificance, made of the horizon a raggedy line.

"May I have a word with you, Uncle?" inquired Phoebe.

"Ah, my dear, I cannot help remarking that the grounds have never looked so well. It is a credit to you, child. You have taken hold in a manner that has exceeded my fondest hopes. I say, will you look at that! London never looks so beautiful but when you are far away from it. Yes, that is exactly how I like

107

the city. Far away and set out like crockery upon a tray. To see it that way, yet to know the congestion and the smoke that is there, gives me pause, and I thank my creator for Pickering Hall and London at a respectable distance."

"I could wish it were closer, your Grace."

"Bah! You do not know what you say! Buildings, one on top of the other, and people so close that one has to share each breath!"

"But at least there are people. By comparison, the Hall is a desert of solitude. Why do we not have more people about? I am sure any of my cousins would be glad to return if we offered some entertainment—a party, perhaps—there might even be some gentlemen and ladies, your neighbors, who would be only too pleased to attend. We could decorate the Hall with pennants and bunting—"

"What in blazes has got into you, Phoebe? Of course we shall not do any such thing! The less I see of my neighbors the better I like 'em! And, I assure you, they are all of them perfect bores—excepting of course those of them that are my particular friends."

"But your friends are so very old!" protested Phoebe.

"I should think that that is only to be expected. I am old and so my friends are old. You do not think for a minute I am about to put up with the silliness and the cavortings and the noise—yes, heaven preserve me from the noise of youth! This is *my* old age, and there is nothing like peace and quiet when one is as old as I."

"But what of me? I am not old, and I am lonely for friends of my own age—"

"That has nothing to say to the necessity of my having to put up with them! I do not see why you cannot be content—but, then again, you are not your Aunt Sophia—now, there was a charming and gracious lady! She was quite content with her lot, quite content to grow old gracefully alongside of me—"

"But she was some three years your senior, Uncle Janus! You cannot expect that of me! It is too soon for me to grow old!"

His Grace sighed. "Well, I suppose you are right. I should have found me someone older—"

"It is not too late!" suggested Phoebe eagerly. "I am sure that Addington could find you some person perfectly suitable and, between himself and me, we could instruct her so quickly to her duties that, in a twinkling, you would find yourself with a housekeeper of sterling character and an absolute paragon—"

"Now, that will be quite enough, Phoebe! We have been all over that ground many times before, and you know that I am more than satisfied to keep you with me. I could never trust this place in any hands but those of a Harewood. After seeing your cousins, I am trebly satisfied that you, my dear, are the only Harewood that could have stood to me in the place of your late sainted aunt."

"But I am not Aunt Sophia, and I am homesick for all that I had in Stevenage—"

"Nonsense! There is nothing that you had in Stevenage that you cannot find in Richmond! How can you even begin to compare the two?"

"But there I had friends and—"

"What, are you a prisoner here? The hill reeks with young people of your age! Don't I hear them shouting the livelong day? Don't they, with their whoophaloos, intrude upon my afternoon naps? And the nights, with their parties and balls! I tell you this neighborhood is going to the dogs! Why the good

Lord ever saw fit to invent young people, I am blessed if I know!"

"But, Uncle Janus, you have just said you will not have them about, so how—"

"And I mean it, Phoebe, every word! I will not tolerate the presence of people who are a day less than five and thirty, and, even then, I think I must be out of my mind to contemplate it. No, if you have a wish for friends of your own age, then I bid you go to them as your duties permit. I say go to them but don't you ever dare to bring a one of them back with you! Now leave me in peace!"

It was not as much as she had wished, but it was more of a concession than she expected, and she was pleased to withdraw from his Grace's presence before he had a chance to change his mind.

The old duke had cause to regret his magnanimity before the week was out. He had not thought, when he had granted Phoebe permission to seek friends in the neighborhood, that she would have been successful in any great rush, but he had not reckoned upon the ingenuity of a lonely young female, especially one so dauntless as his niece.

The very next day, Phoebe had ordered out the carriage, and, after having made sure with Addington that the household was well-ordered to see to the comfort of its master, she had driven out to make a round of calls. Since his Grace had not recognized the necessity of providing her with her own calling cards, she had coolly helped herself to some of his, and they served her very well indeed.

The lords and ladies resident upon Richmond Hill and in its environs had long given up any hope of making more than a nodding acquaintance with

Grade of Pickering Hall, and to have this fresh young lady burst in upon them, who turned out to be no less than the successor to Lady Harewood, they were overwhelmed by the honor. Phoebe had no trouble in garnering a fistful of invitations not only to call again, but to attend any number of routs and parties then being arranged. There was a push to return her courtesy with calls upon his Grace at Pickering Hall. This Phoebe easily discouraged by saying that the duke was not in any case to receive company—which certainly was true enough!

When day after day passed, and the duke could never find her to air his eternal complaints, and when evening after evening passed with only Phoebe's empty plate at the dinner table to keep him company, his Grace was fit to be tied. It was disgraceful that the Mistress of Pickering Hall should be forever gallivanting about the neighborhood! It just was not to be tolerated! Sophia had never done such a thing! Never would she have thought to abandon her brother to his own devices; never would she have failed to be about, to hear his complaints; never, not ever, had she failed to make her appearance at dinner!

The duke was filled with indignation at this untoward behaviour in his housekeeper and more. Not that he would have ever admitted it to a soul, but he was finding that Phoebe's presence had become more for him than a mere convenience. He had got a true fondness for the girl, a fondness not at all diminished by his pride in her. At the beginning, her challenging him at every turn had been a source of great annoyance, for it was a thing he was not used to. No one challenged Grade! But she had, and she had held her own against him quite well indeed, and in a way that

111

Sophia had never achieved. Where his sister had been sweet and forbearing, Phoebe had not hesitated to make her opinion known, and rare it was that she had bowed meekly to his arbitrariness. He had come to like that in her, and it was a source of wonder to him that he even tolerated it, for he could not imagine himself accepting such disrespect from any other person.

The business of her leaving Pickering Hall every day exercised his wrath, but he was at a loss as to how he was to put a stop to it. He had given his permission, and he could hardly retract it for anything but an exceptional reason, and that he was hard put to find. The little minx had got Addington and the rest of the household so under her thumb that the Hall ran itself perfectly even in her absence. All his complaints of late had been of no validity, he knew, and had only served to make Phoebe pay him some attention.

He felt very irritable these days. He had been outfoxed, at long last, and by a mere slip of a girl. He had never thought he should live to see the day.

Late one afternoon his Grace was seated out upon the lawn under a parasol that had been set to keep the sun away, but as the sun was now approaching the horizon, it shone fully upon the duke, casting an orange glow about him, which he never noticed, as he gazed peacefully at the vista before him. The look of deep concentration on his face was brought about by the problem that had been exercising his faculties for many a day. He was not used to being alone so much. It was of little satisfaction to keep Addington nearby, the man had little conversation, and, anyway, his Grace found it impossible to address the fellow in any but the surliest of tones. Addington, for all his fine qualities as butler, did not strike a chord with the duke.

The depth of his concentration was attested to by the fact that Addington was now in the process of clearing his throat for the third time in an attempt to penetrate the duke's brown study.

"Dammit, man, I wish you would do something for your throat!" exclaimed his Grace in annoyance.

"Er—I beg your pardon, your Grace, I shall have it attended to immediately. May I inquire if your Grace will receive a caller?"

Tearing his eyes from the distant towers of London, the duke wheeled in his chair and glared at Addington. "Are you daft, man? At this hour? Why it is nigh on to the dinner hour! And where may I ask is Miss Phoebe? Has she got a home here anymore?"

"Miss Phoebe is gone to tea with Lady Leamington, your Grace."

"She was invited, do you say?"

"So I am told, your Grace."

"And never a word to me, Grade? Are there no manners left in this world? Does not rank count for precedence any longer? Am I, the head of the house of Harewood, to be ignored while the most insignificant member of my family and my household is given every consideration before me? Ah, it shall not be! I say it shall not be! Never shall a Leamington set foot under my roof, I can tell you!"

Addington blinked. He was quite sure that the Prince Regent himself would never have dared to venture forth into Pickering Hall, much less any of the Leamingtons.

"Who's the fellow?" demanded his Grace.

"Er—the fellow, your Grace?" asked Addington thoroughly shaken and confused.

"Well, damme, you did inform me that someone was calling upon me! Who is the infernal shuttlehead with such gall to call upon me at this hour?"

"It is a Captain Maitland, your Grace. Here is his card."

The old gentleman grumpily snatched the pasteboard from Addington's hand and scanned it as he muttered: "Captain Maitland? I have no acquaintance in the navy—an army captain? I know a general or two, but a mere captain? Oh, I say! It is *Brent Maitland*! Well, why did you not say so in the first place, you numbskull? He is my great-nephew! What's he doing in the army—and what is that scapegrace doing *here* of all places? I suppose he heard that there was a death in the family and thinks to collect his inheritance. Well, I am not dead yet, as he shall soon see! Fetch him to me, Addington! He is in for a surprise, I am sure, and one he'll not savor!"

Addington quickly decamped. In a few moments he returned leading a tall officer of striking appearance, garbed in his regimentals. As soon as the young man caught sight of the duke, he came rapidly up to him and took his unwilling hand which he proceeded to shake, crying: "Uncle Janus, how very good to see you! You are looking marvellously well!"

"That is all you know! I look like the jaws of death—but do not take heart, for I am not yet ready, by far, to surrender up the title to you!"

"I should hope not, Uncle Janus! Indeed, it was a great shock to me to learn of Aunt Sophia's being taken. That is why I have come. I did not like the thought of you being all alone in this great house."

"How touching!" exclaimed the duke sourly. "I am

114

sure it will please you to learn that I am not all alone in this great house, and you can just turn around and carry yourself back to London. Two Harewoods are as much as this place can endure!"

Captain Maitland laughed. "Well, it is good to see that you have not changed, your Grace—but surely this is no proper courtesy to your heir."

"I never made you my heir, rot you!—and how is it that I was never informed of your taking a commission in the army, may I ask?"

The captain looked uncomfortable. "As a matter of fact, I did not take a commission. I went in as a private soldier. I gained my rank before the enemy, you see—"

"What?" shouted his Grace. "A Harewood in the ranks? How utterly disgraceful! How dared you to drag our illustrious name down to such degradation?"

"Well, as it happened, I was a bit short of the ready and—well, it was worse than that. You see, I had a few creditors, and France looked a likely refuge—Sir, you'd never have raised a finger to ease me out of a sponging house—"

"Clever boy!" agreed his Grace with a malicious smile. "I'd have let you rot, you good-for-nothing! Spend! Spend! Spend! That is all you know! The day of reckoning will never come!—you think! I say it is damnably unfair that I, Grade, should be cursed with such an heir as you?"

"Well, you need not look at me that way. I had nothing to do with it either!" retorted the captain heatedly. "Uncle, I did not come to hear the very same lecture you have been reading me all my life—"

"No, you did not, I am sure. You came because London is a little hot for you. I daresay it is the debtor's side of Newgate for you, my lad, if they ever

115

catch up with you. You should have stayed on in France with the occupation—or kept on travelling. Richmond is but a stone's throw from London, you know. I daresay the runners are hot on your tail."

"Well, dammit, a captain's pay does not go very far! And, furthermore, as the scion of Harewood, one would think you, with all of the Harewood wealth in your possession, would see me better off. I am not the only fellow with prospects in the service, Uncle, but one would think that I had the least of any of them. I am Grade's heir—and a sorry specimen it makes of me!"

"Bah! Cease your bawling before you unman me! Aye, you are a sorry specimen, indeed! To go for a common soldier! The least you could have done was to apply to me for the money to purchase a commission and go into the service like a gentleman!"

That evoked a burst of hearty laughter from the captain. "Well now, Uncle, if I had been assured of your assistance in the matter, I'd not have had to go in the first place. The purchase money would have been enough to get the bloodsuckers off my back! Just think how much money I did save you! I have got me a commission for nothing and come out of the army like a gentleman even if I did not go in that way."

The old man eyed his great-nephew shrewdly. "Well, at least you do not blow upon your exploits."

His nephew eyed his great-uncle just as shrewdly. "Why should I? You would only remark that it was no more than was to be expected of a Harewood."

"You are as impertinent as ever! One could have hoped that the service would have taught you respect for rank."

"Uncle Janus, I am returned! Who is that with you?" called out Phoebe from the gathering dusk.

116

"Well, young lady, my cup runneth over with avuncular ecstasy! Pray do not tell me I am to have the honor of your company this evening, for I am sure I must faint away with the shock of it."

"But, Uncle, you never said anything to make me believe my presence was any better than a necessary bother to you," she remarked as she came up to them."

"Yes, well, your Aunt Sophia never failed to dine with me whatever my thinking—"

Captain Maitland stepped closer to Phoebe and stared into her face.

"I say," he exclaimed. "Uncle, I pray you will do the honors."

"Phoebe, this is your cousin, quite removed, and the farther the better. My heir, blast him! Brent Maitland. He'll not be staying—"

"Well, for dinner at least, Uncle! I am famished and have ridden hard—"

"I'll wager you have! Shall we set a cover or two for the runners?"

"—to see you, your Grace, and a fine dinner surely ought to be mine to ameliorate the unpleasantness of your august company."

"I'll give you unpleasantness, you overgrown whippersnapper! Phoebe, against my inclinations, we are to have a guest to dinner."

"Yes, Uncle," said Phoebe, quietly, as she eyed the captain. "I am sure we are delighted to have him."

"I say, Uncle, that is a very pretty niece you have got!" exclaimed Captain Maitland. "May I inquire from which side of the family you stole her?"

"Phoebe is a Harewood, just as you, except she does credit to the name. She is daughter to my niece, Lydia, who married the Grantham fellow."

117

"I am quite in accord with you, sir, on that. I knew there were some female Harewoods about, but she must certainly stand out from all of them, I vow."

Phoebe was blushing, but she retorted: "Then you have not met with Fredericka!"

He looked directly at her as he retorted: "Ah, Cousin, but I have!"

It was now too dusky to discern if Phoebe's blushes grew deeper.

Growled the duke: "Rake! Do not listen to the fellow, Phoebe! He is a silver-tongued devil, a lady-killer without a feather to fly with. No doubt you have gone through your expectations and think to touch me for your room and board," remarked the duke as he turned to the captain.

"Well, Uncle, in one way you are right, but in another you are quite wrong—but, I say, must we continue to converse in the dark? Surely you can afford a candle or two in the Hall to light the scene. I would gaze upon my cousin, sir."

"Excuse me, Uncle. I must inform Addington that we have a guest to dinner," said Phoebe, and she left them for the house.

"I say, will she be about for a while?"

"She happens to be my housekeeper, Maitland," snapped his Grace.

"Do you mean to say that that young lady is filling Aunt Sophia's shoes?"

"Surely, you can put it more delicately than that," complained the duke. "What do you mean, I am right and I am wrong? Say plainly what you mean."

"I have not borrowed a penny on my expectations—"

"So you do have a spark of decency left in you—"

118

"But only because I was sure that somehow you would see me through!"

"The devil I shall!"

"Uncle, it is not nice to turn your heir out upon his uppers and he a war hero, too. I know you care not a ha' penny for your reputation, but it would be an insult to your beloved country to do in a man who has been mentioned in the dispatches three times."

"Now, you have gone too far, Nephew! For such feats as you imply, you would merit the Order of the Bath. You are an empty braggart after all! It was to be expected."

They had been strolling together towards the Hall. Now they ascended the stairs and came into the entryway flooded with light.

"Since my credit with you, gracious Uncle, could not be at a lower ebb, I have no hesitancy in admitting our sovereign was foolish enough to have conferred upon me that order."

"And of course, there was no room or thought for Grade at the ceremony of investiture. How do you dare show your face to me? Never a word of such a signal honor paid to a Harewood! Forget the miserable, poor old duke! For this cut I am to feed you?"

"There was no ceremony and probably never will be, Uncle, so you can climb down out of the boughs now. The exigencies of the campaign, don't you know. I had a bit of hot work to do and couldn't be spared. It was announced in the *Gazette,* and that will have to do."

"So it is Sir Brent, is it?"

"Aye, knight commander."

"Wouldn't you know that the first K. C. B. for the Harewoods has to be a Maitland! Why could not the Harewoods have produced males when it counted."

119

"I say, Uncle, are you never satisfied?"

"Stop your impertinence and go to your rooms and change for dinner! I'll send my valet to you."

"Believe me, your Grace, but I have managed quite well without one these past few years; however, I have not the vaguest idea of where my rooms are."

"Addington will know. I shall ring for him to show you up—but don't get too comfortable in them for you are not staying!"

"But, your Grace—"

"Enough! Ah, here is Addington! I shall leave you in his hands."

Chapter X

PHOEBE was something pensive as Buckle helped her dress for dinner.

"My, Miss Phoebe, but haven't we been going about! Lately, it is lucky I am to get a sight of you before bedtime. I do not think the master, his Grace, is particularly pleased."

"Oh, has he said anything to indicate his displeasure?"

"That is just it. He does not say anything. Why, he has not whigged Addington for days, and we go about on tippy toes expecting him to go off in a temper at any moment He has not fired a one of us this past week. Oh, 'tis most ominous, I am thinking."

"Well, he can start his complaints now, for I am home. I daresay my ears will be bent to a fare-thee-well—but I don't care! I am getting out and meeting with our neighbors, and that is a deal more pleasant a diversion than any I have had of late."

"Have you been meeting any fine gentlemen, might I ask, Miss Phoebe?"

"Oh, a few, but I do not think that they understand that I am his Grace's poor relation. If they had the least notion, I am sure I should never be as welcome as I am—but let that be sufficient to the day. I am having a most enjoyable time, and that is all that matters."

"Er—the gentleman come to dinner—he is a might young to be a guest of his Grace."

"Oh, that is no gentleman! He is Captain Brent Maitland, his Grace's heir—and of course a distant cousin of mine, don't you know."

"I did not get but a glimpse of him. He appeared to be a gentleman of parts and very handsome in that uniform. Has he been to France?"

"So I gathered," Phoebe responded absently. "Yes, he is handsome," she mused. "Especially in that uniform," she added hastily.

"There now!" exclaimed Buckle. "I think that's got it!"

She stepped back as Phoebe went to the full-length mirror and examined her appearance. She cocked her head, first one way, then the other, and ended by shaking it in disapproval.

"No. No, it will not do, Buckle. It looks so—so ordinary, I am thinking."

"Why, his Grace complimented you in it once!"

"Yes, but then his Grace's taste in ladies' gowns is more attuned to what my late aunt, Sophia, might have worn, and she must have been thrice my age. No, take out that party dress that I have worn but once. I brought it with me thinking his Grace would be giving at least one ball for his nieces—How utterly foolish that notion seems now—Ah, yes, the very one! Help me out of this, Buckle, and let us see what justice that heavenly creation will do for me."

"Yes, Miss Phoebe," replied Buckle, busily assisting her. "But I do not understand the necessity for a new dress this evening. Oh, is it that Mr. Maitland who is the cause? But he is your relative."

"Buckle, it is Captain Maitland, and he is not all that close a relation to me. In fact, this is the first time I have laid eyes on the gentleman—but that is not to say that I am wearing anything special for *his* benefit. Not at all! It is just that the poor fellow is all bound up in that uniform of his, and I would put him at ease by appearing in attire to suit—merely what any thoughtful hostess might do."

"Of course, Miss Phoebe."

But it was the thoughtful hostess who found herself not at ease, for, when the gentlemen made their appearance in the dining room, the captain was clad in mufti, and there was not the least sign of the military in his apparel. He looked a perfectly ordinary gentleman, a perfectly ordinary but very handsome gentleman, that is to say.

Her overdressed appearance did not escape the duke's eye. He gave her a quizzical look and exclaimed: "May I inquire what is the occasion for such a display, my dear? It is only a distant cousin we are showing our favor to this evening."

"It is all that I could find to wear, Uncle Janus," she began to explain.

"Well now, Cousin Harewood, I assure you I cannot see a thing wrong. You do it perfect justice, and I am overwhelmed!" With that Brent came to her and raised her hand to his lips with a smile.

"Brent, put it down and behave yourself!" snapped his Grace.

"Of course, sir, but with the greatest reluctance."

He edged Addington aside and helped Phoebe with her chair.

As he took his own seat, the duke, at the head of the table, looked at Phoebe and then at the captain.

123

From the thoughtful look upon his face it was obvious that he was trying to come to a conclusion of sorts.

As Addington signaled for the meal to be served, his Grace turned to Phoebe and remarked: "It seems to me, young lady, that you are definitely overdressed for the occasion, and you should take better care of your clothes so that you do not run out of proper attire. Of course, if you insist upon calling upon everyone and his cousin every blessed day, the laundresses will never be up with you—"

"Uncle, since she is your charge, why not just buy her clothes sufficient to her needs. Heaven knows you can afford it," helpfully suggested the captain.

His Grace glared at him and retorted: "You, Nephew, keep you nose out of my affairs until I am dead and they become your own."

"No, your Grace, I do not care to wait that long."

"What do you mean?" demanded the duke.

"Oh, I beg your pardon. I fear I was thinking out loud," Brent replied, all confusion.

"If that is a sample of your thinking, I marvel that no one has investigated your sanity by this time. Ah, René has done himself proud this evening, I see. That looks like a very tender saddle of lamb—and about time!"

Considering that his Grace was at best begrudgingly hospitable to his nephew, the meal went along quite well. Brent proved a charming and voluble speaker, ever ready to respond openly to any questions put to him concerning how he had been spending the past few years of his life. Since that must have concerned the adventures of the army in France against Napoleon, Phoebe was fascinated to hear all

124

she could. Her interest in current events proved intense.

The duke wore a scowl and took no part in the table talk, but that is not to say that he was not listening, and attentively, to the exchange that was going on between his niece and nephew. Not only was he listening to their every word, but he was studying their facial expressions as well. Whatever he was thinking, his scowl never left his face.

Captain Sir Brent Maitland, K. C. B., was the oddest sort of ranker, one must suppose, and his experiences in Wellington's expeditionary force bore it out. As an enlisted man, his superiors experienced the greatest difficulty giving his orders, knowing full well they were addressing a future Duke of Grade—and of course no gentleman-ranker was he, as no disgrace was connected with his name. They could not believe that he had enlisted because he was fresh out of funds and heavily in debt—not he, the heir of Grade! They attributed his being amongst them in such a humble rank to his liking for a lark and advanced him up the ranks just as rapidly as they could, much to the relief of the noncommissioned officers who had to deal with him directly.

But that only made matters worse, for Sergeant Maitland was always amongst the first to volunteer for an assignment, and that brought him in even greater contact with his officers who believed him to be their social superior. Reasoning that had he been truly a duke's son, he would have born the courtesy title of marquis, the commanding general of the sector, in collusion with the rest of his staff, assigned the sergeant to lieutenant colonel who happened to be an earl, the highest noble rank they had in the command. This did not make the earl happy in the least.

He was but the eldest son of a marquis and bore his title by courtesy. It was a worry to everyone as to who had the precedence, and earl, by courtesy, or the commoner, heir to the title of duke.

So upsetting was this question to the officer corps, that the progress of the campaign was threatened, and an appeal was made to Wellington to transfer the troublesome sergeant to the staff of a duke. Wellington, having but recently been raised to that station himself, and being the only duke handy, was not about to be bothered with such idiocy and, in a fit of temper, shot back a reply to put the bastard before the enemy. If he got himself killed, the problem was solved, and, if they made sure to put him where the enemy was making it hot for them and the fellow survived, he'd commission him directly, and that, too, would solve their problem.

Such a judgement of Solomon was not to be ignored, and, for a bit, Brent had got his fill of action before the enemy. Not only had he survived, but he had taken over the company when all the officers had fallen and managed it so well that Wellington was overjoyed to see the problem solved so nicely. On the basis of other brilliantly fought actions, Brent rose rapidly to the rank of captain by the time Napoleon had received his final discomfiture.

He elected to stay on with the army of occupation rather than return to his poverty-stricken former existence in and about London, and things in France quieted down until the army started to strip itself of its wartime enrollment. By that time Brent had had enough and refused a promotion to major, deciding it was time he began to take his prospective succession seriously.

Having reached this point in his narrative, he

turned to his uncle and remarked: "Now do you see how deceived you were in your judgement of me, my Uncle? I am come to grace your declining years and learn first hand the business of being a duke. You will admit I have been given damn little opportunity to get used to the idea."

"That has got to be the most fatuous excuse I have ever heard to batten upon an old man's hospitality!" exclaimed his Grace. "You are expecting me to support you in style, you, my successor, the one man who will perform cartwheels over my grave with joy at my being taken? Hah!"

"Oh, Uncle, how bad of you to think that of me! Cartwheels are such childish capers! No, I was thinking of something more sedate, a display of fireworks, perhaps," he said with a grin.

Phoebe chuckled.

"And I suppose, Miss, you would be only too happy to light them off!"

"But of course I would not, Uncle." She paused as the old man's countenance lighted up a bit. Then she added: "I am too frightened of the nasty things. I should let Addington light them and watch the celebration from a safe distance!"

The duke's scowl returned, but he could not maintain it and snorted in reluctant laughter.

He declared: "So you have got yourself an adherent to your cause, I see. Well, I am not to be taken in so easily. I dare say you are quite an expensive fellow, even to start. Pray inform me what you are going to cost me when Bow Street comes aknocking on our door?"

"Uncle, I wish you would not put it like that. You make it sound so unfriendly. We are related, you know."

"Don't I though! Do you think I could ever forget?"

"It can hardly hurt you to support your heir in reasonable style. It is no more than is done in other families."

"It is hardly any excuse for the Harewoods to indulge in such nonsense just because others do. Why, you are not even my son, merely a distant relative and a poor one at that!"

Brent chortled. "Aye, I am distant all right—at least twice removed, I'd venture to guess, but I am your closest male relative, and, as for being poor, that is a state I share with the rest of our exalted family."

"I suppose you expect me to confer one of my titles upon you, too, by way of courtesy."

"I certainly would have no objection if you were so moved."

"Well, I am not so moved! Thank your stars and my benevolence that I permit you to stay on at Pickering Hall—that is, if the price is not too high. What do you owe?"

"Oh, I daresay the runners can be got off my tail for something less than a cow—"

"A thousand?"

Even Phoebe was shocked at the mention of such a huge sum.

"You do forget, Uncle, that I have been living upon my uppers for going on five years. A captain's pay is not so much, but a sergeant's is a deal less! What would you have me do? I am a gentleman, and, what is more, heir to Grade!"

"So I, Grade, am to blame, I take it."

"In a manner of speaking, yes! I was never asked if I wished to be your successor, so I can hardly be blamed if the distinction without some emolument is distinctly galling to me."

"And how galling must it be to me to see all that I have so carefully preserved pass into the hands of one who is practically a stranger to me?"

"Oh, I should not take on so if I were you, Uncle. You will not have to stay around to witness it, I am sure," Brent said with a smile.

His Grace snorted and brought his napkin quickly up to his lips to hide the smile that formed there irresistibly.

"Well, I shall arrange to see your debts settled. Phoebe, remind me to see to it tomorrow."

"Uncle, your generosity is matched only by your pleasant disposition."

"Flattery, young man, will get you nowhere!" snapped his Grace with a sparkle of humor in his eyes.

"Now, I pray you will tell me, Brent, what you proposed to do in the event that I was adamant upon this issue?"

"Oh, I should have left the country for America. There, being heir to Grade would have been no disadvantage. I could have found a living of some sort, and no one would have looked askance at me."

"But that would be to lower yourself! How very demeaning to even think of going into trade!"

"Trade? I should say not! I picked up the rudiments of surveying in my service. I would have gone out into the American wilderness where the demand for surveyors must be fabulous."

"Bah! That is still a trade and beneath a gentleman, not to say a Harewood in line to be a duke!"

"I assure you, Uncle, in America it cannot be a trade. Indeed, it has got to be a most respectable profession. General Washington began his career as a surveyor!"

129

"Is that your ambition? To become a president for a pack of colonials?"

"Well, I am sure there is something more that is required than being a surveyor to become a president in the United States of America, your Grace."

"Well, it is all a piece of nonsense! You could never have got there in the first place. If you need a thousand pounds here in England, where would you have found the money for your passage?" asked the duke triumphantly.

"I should have gone aboard as a seaman and worked for my passage."

"Oh, my stars, you would never have done any such thing, Cousin!" exclaimed Phoebe in horror.

Brent laughed. "Do not exercise yourself so, Cousin. I am not in any danger of so abasing myself, thanks to Uncle Janus."

"Brent, you are not fit to be a duke!" exclaimed his Grace. "I wonder that you even pretend to be a gentleman with such notions."

Brent bowed his head towards the duke. "I am sure your Grace will see to it that I am instructed in all those graces and opinions necessary for a proper duke."

"Egad, that will take more than my natural life, I am sure! Heaven forfend that I should be saddled with you for the rest of my days! That prospect turns the very food to gall in my mouth! I shall retire to the reading room and ease the taste with some good brandy. Good night to you!"

With a gesture of disgust, the duke arose from the table and threw down his serviette. "Before I go, I would ask you, Phoebe, where are you off to on the morrow?"

"Oh, Uncle Janus, I had thought to go to—but, no, I

am sure I shall not. There are things requiring my attention at the Hall. I—I shall be quite occupied seeing to them tomorrow."

He merely nodded and strode out of the room, as usual forgetting his walking stick. As he passed out the door, his features broke into a grin of satisfaction.

Chapter XI

A RATHER AMAZING THING occurred the next morning. His Grace did not put in an appearance for breakfast. Sending down word that he was a bit indisposed, he had his breakfast brought to him in his bedroom. Full of concern, Phoebe went up to him to consult with him about the necessity of calling in a physician. However indisposed the duke might have felt, nothing could be determined from his disposition; it was as grumpy as ever. He refused outright any medical attention and admonished her not to bother herself about him, to keep an eye on his nephew instead. "I'll not put it past that scoundrel to make off with the family plate!" he growled.

Phoebe assured him that Brent was an officer and a gentleman and would never stoop to such base conduct.

His Grace declared that any gentleman worthy of the name would never have stooped to becoming an enlisted man in the service and shooed her out.

Phoebe was much relieved to see the old man so up to his usual form and went down to see to the household arrangements and entertain her guest. The household required very little of her attention, so that she was pleased to seek out Brent to inquire as to his comfort and convenience as a proper hostess was bound to do.

She found him seated in her uncle's favorite chair in the reading room, the chair, that, by the dint of numerous cleanings and airings, had finally been restored to its former unredolent state.

Brent arose immediately upon her entering and said in greeting: "You keep a most excellent establishment, Cousin. His Grace is a most fortunate man."

"Thank you, Cousin. I thought to inquire if there is any special dish you would like our chef to prepare for dinner."

"He would not by any chance happen to be French?"

"Oh dear, I forgot! Indeed he is! I do not suppose you are particularly fond of anything French, are you"

"*Au contraire, ma cherie,* I love all things French! Their wo—er—wines are nectar, and their dishes are culinary delights! Can he really prepare platters *a la francaise?*"

"And very well, indeed! René is superb and would like nothing better than to cook for someone who can appreciate his art. Indeed, as his Grace has no particular fondness for the finer things that René adores to make, I have constituted myself a gourmet to make the poor man happy. Some of the things he makes for me are so rich, it would be a favor to me if you would relieve me of the burden."

"My pleasure, Cousin. Do take me down to the fellow, and I will make known to him my appreciation of the dishes of his country. Um—yes, perhaps he would like to start with some fowl done up in wine and a bit of fish *tartare,* nothing fancy, but definitely in the French style, don't you know."

René, an old monarchist and, therefore, completely out of sympathy with the unsurper, looked upon Brent from the start as *"le sauveur de ma patrie, La Belle France!"* and nothing of his efforts was too good for *le brave Capitane* Mai'lon'. Phoebe thought Brent hit it off quite nicely with the temperamental Frenchman and was truly surprised at the good-fellowship that sprung up between two such different persons, especially in light of the recent fracas between their two countries.

Brent came away from the kitchen with her all chuckles, remarking: "If you can swallow a Frenchie's inordinate vanity, you can get him to do anything for you!"

They did not stay in the house, for it was a beautiful day outside, and it seemed the most natural thing to go out in the gardens for a stroll and conversation. Whatever the reason, that is precisely where they wound up, and Phoebe began to take Brent to task.

"Cousin, what you said about Frenchmen below stairs is just as true of the English, if you will just give it some thought—and I could wish you would apply some of that philosophy to your present benefactor. Must you be forever at his Grace's throat. I do not believe you showed the slightest respect nor have you been anything but vitriolic in your remarks to him. After all, he is Grade, and the head of the Harewoods to boot."

"I merely gave him as good as I got—but do not worry yourself about it, it is an old story between us. I cannot remember if ever he has had a kind or an encouraging word for me. I did not expect him to bow down and kiss the floor at my feet, but surely my accomplishments in the service were hardly grounds for complaint."

"But that is his way, don't you see? When you are his age, and you will be Grade yourself then, if you have a wish to be a crabby, you will be crabby and think nothing of it, wait and see."

"Well, as I have no choice in the matter, I shall certainly have to, won't I? But you are not to take our exchanges all that seriously, Cousin. I do not."

"Well, I cannot help but. To see two people for whom I have a familial affection constantly exchanging insults is most disheartening, I assure you, Cousin."

"Sweet Cousin, far be it from me to cause you the least anguish. For the familial affection I bear you, I shall mend my ways and be all that is respectful and proper to his Grace."

"I am happy to hear you say so. Uncle Janus has a temper, and he just might lose it some day with you and off to the Americas you will go and—and I just hate the idea of you laboring on the decks, a common ordinary seaman. That would be awfully bad of you!" she scolded.

"I have done worse work in my time. It would not faze me."

"I am not thinking of you! I am thinking of myself! What do you think it is like for me here with never a body of my own age to converse with? Do you think I will be overcome with joy to see you depart?"

"Well, come to think of it, I am not so sure I will be laughing if it should come to pass, either. I say, Cousin, I do not feel very cousinly to you."

Phoebe chortled. "If the fact be known, I find it very difficult to think of you as I do of my four cousins."

"Well, I should hope not! They are all of them females, are they not?"

"Oh, now you are being silly! What I mean to say

is that we are practically perfect strangers. We are meeting here for the very first time. Until now you were naught to me but a shadowy name."

"I cannot return you even that much of a compliment. My cousins Harewood were never more to me than a remote connection about whose names I never bothered to inquire—I shall never forget yours, Phoebe."

"But you did meet with Fredericka? You said you did."

"Aye, but it was ages ago, and I do not recall the occasion. She is quite a beauty, but the attic is to let," he said, grinning, and tapping his forehead."

Phoebe chuckled. "Yes, and the lack of wits in the others proved to be my downfall."

"What do you mean, your downfall?" asked Brent suddenly quite concerned.

"It is the reason for my being here, housekeeper to Uncle Janus."

"I should hardly consider that post to be anything less than an honor," he protested.

"Oh, I quite agree it is an honor but one I would rather do without, for it is certainly no pleasure. How much would you like to be pent up with the old man, day after day, having to listen to his eternal complaining and never able to entertain for a moment the prospect of fun and gaiety?"

"I am sure I should make a very indifferent sort of housekeeper," he teased. "But I have seen that he acts to you with all due respect and suspect that you are your own mistress here."

"Well, that is true enough, but it was not something he gave in to easily, you may be sure."

"So you, too, have words with the old reprobate occasionally?"

"He can be quite impossible, but that is not to say that we bicker at every opportunity as you seem intent upon doing, Cousin."

"Now, do not nag at me. I have given you my promise to behave with him in the future, and I shall keep to it—but what then do you have to complain of, my dear? You come and go as you please, do you not?"

"Yes, but it is not the same! It was all well and good for Aunt Sophia to be content with this lot, for she was old and life had passed her by ages ago, but I am not ready to retire from the world! Let some one else have the honor, for I see it only as an encumbrance. Other young ladies of my age have no need to concern themselves with the state of the pantry and feed for the stables. If they have any such concerns at all, it is for their own little households and for their husbands, those of them that have married. With Pickering Hall attached to me like a ball and chain, I shall never be married!" she lamented.

He nodded his head solemnly. "It is only too true. You must abandon all hope. Life has passed you by, and you remain eternally on the shelf. How long has it been, do you think?"

She gave him an odd look and asked: "How long has what been?"

"How long has it been since your hand was asked for?"

She shook her head crossly. "No one has ever made me an offer!"

He shook his head mournfully. "As bad as all that! My, my! and you already past the age of sixteen. Oh, believe me, dear Cousin, my heart goes out to you."

"I am past seventeen, and you are quizzing me, Cousin!"

He laughed. "Well, just look about you, and you cannot blame me! What is there so bad here to make you blue? You are surrounded by luxury and wealth. You are your own mistress—and at an age few females can expect that. To worry yourself into the mopes over a wedding that may well befall you long before you qualify for spinster is nonsensical in the extreme."

"Oh, do you think it is so easy? Do you think that all this wealth will not be a hindrance rather than an inducement to a prospective suitor—for you must know that should I leave here, I would take nothing with me—not even his Grace's good wishes."

"Well, you could leave if you had a mind to it, couldn't you?"

"If I did not count the cost, I could. But Uncle Janus would not hesitate to cut my family and myself out of any further consideration, and that must make my chances for a decent marriage dim beyond perception. I might just as well stay on with him."

She paused for a moment and then looked up with a glint in her eye. "Pray tell me, Cousin, how do *you* view my prospects? Do *you* see me as a wife?"

He reared back a bit and looked her up and down. Then he put his hands in his pockets and began to circle her slowly, giving her a thorough going-over with his eyes. Phoebe bit her lip and blushed.

"Brent, I did not mean *you*, for heaven's sake!"

"Oh, sorry, my dear. I thought you might be proposing to me," he said, coming about and continuing to stroll along with her.

"No, no, what I mean to say is, who could have the least interest in a duke's housekeeper?"

"I should imagine another duke, don't you think? Speaking of which, as I have some reasonable expectation in just that direction, I shall certainly keep your proposal in mind. After all, you, better than any one, has to be the best qualified to look after Pickering Hall, which, by a strange circumstance, is exactly where I shall be residing when that distant future fate befalls me."

"Well, you shall have to find someone else, Cousin, for I do not intend to be here in that distant future!"

"How sad! Well, in the meantime, I shall certainly keep my eye out for a duke for you to wed. Do you have any preference as to age or wealth, my dear?"

Phoebe chuckled. "You never let up, do you? It is all sheer fun as you see it. Wait, my good sir, just you wait, and you will see how much fun it can be living under the same roof with Uncle Janus. By the way, how long do you intend to stay on with us?"

"Until the old boy throws me out. I hope he does not, but it will not be all that bad. Once he has reestablished my credit, I should be able to live on tick for another few years."

Phoebe frowned. "I should not blame him if he did send you packing. He can hardly care to be reminded of the succession and what it means to him at every sight of you lolling about."

Brent shrugged his shoulders. "What else would you have me do? I am a gentleman of such prospects that it would be unthinkable for me to put myself in trade. Politics is for the wealthy or the toadies, and even the latter must have some sort of an independence. If I move about in society, I must do it on wealth or at least the appearance of wealth. That means the gaming tables, mistresses, and all that brainless business of dandyism and sport. After Waterloo, I see it all as a childish bore and elect to spend my time in the company of my ferocious uncle and my adorable cousin. What is so bad as that??"

140

"Well, you had better make that your ferocious uncle, for your adorable cousin has not the time. I have a household to run and plans to make if I am ever to escape from Pickering Hall."

"Now that may be interesting to hear. What plans have you made thus far?"

"None whatsoever. I am at point-non-plus. Uncle Janus has me defeated on all sides."

"You know, Cousin, I just might be able to give you a bit of assistance in that direction. After all, when it comes to strategy, I rather pride myself in that I have done a bit of it in my time and done it well. I hardly think that Uncle Janus is so fearsome an opponent as was Napoleon."

Phoebe's eyebrows came up. "I did not know I was addressing the Duke of Wellington, your Grace!"

Brent laughed. "Now, come, let us be serious. You have an objective to gain, your freedom from Pickering Hall and you are being foiled by your enemy, Uncle Janus. In short, you have got all the elements of a military action facing you. The problem: to defeat his Grace without losing your standing with him. Is not that the gist of the situation?"

"You make it sound so simple. I assure you it is not."

"Be that as it may, I can see that you are not making any headway with it and am offering you my assistance. I'll give you odds that I should have no trouble handling the old boy myself, in my own behalf; but I can see where you might not be so free to deal with him as I am, and, therefore, I say you need my help in the matter."

Phoebe looked at him doubtfully. "I do not see how you can do anything but make matters worse. Uncle Janus holds you at arms length even now. Were you

141

to champion me, I cannot see that it would gain me a thing."

"Well, there is not the slightest need for me to become openly involved. What I am suggesting is that we put our heads together and analyze the situation, discover our strengths and his Grace's weaknesses. It then is merely a matter of exerting ourselves against him where he cannot protect himself."

"Uncle Janus has no weaknesses!"

"Naploeon thought as much for himself and see what happened to him!" retorted Brent. "Anyway, two heads are better than one, and it is better to try than to sit about forever all despondent."

Phoebe thought about it for a moment. "Well, perhaps you are right. At any rate, I shall think about it. In the meantime, I have got work to do and shall have to take my leave of you."

"I am looking forward to our council of war, Cousin. I am sure I never was so eager for those we held in France as I am for this one."

"If you can help me in this, I shall be forever grateful."

"I'll spend this day with his Grace, reconnoitering the enemy, as it were, and what say we put our heads together tomorrow morning?"

"There are some special purchases I needs must make in Richmond then—"

"Excellent. I shall drive you, and it will be a perfect time for us to conspire."

Chapter XII

RICHMOND TOWN was no great distance from Pickering Hall, but the road did not descend directly down to it. If one took one's time about it, the drive could occupy all of twenty-five minutes as the way slowly circled about the broad rise that was Richmond Hill—and if one were to digress from the road and enter upon the grounds of the beautiful park open to the public, a half day could easily be spent in going from Pickering Hall down to the town.

At the stables there had been some debate as to who was to hold the reins of the gig that was a particular favorite of Phoebe's. As Mistress of Pickering Hall, Phoebe quite outranked Captain Maitland, K. C. B., and he, never having had the questionable pleasure of being driven about by a female, gave it to her in good grace, even chuckling as he mounted up to the left side of the seat.

As soon as they had passed out of the gates to the estate, Sir Brent began to say: "I have been giving a deal of thought to your situation, my dear—"

"No, wait, Brent, until we have got to the park. There we can tarry a while and talk quite freely. It is quite a beautiful place and has a view of London to compare with that of which Uncle Janus is so proud."

"Very well, I would not wish to take your attention from your driving."

Phoebe gave him a disdainful look and flicked the reins. The horse surged forward at a smart trot, and, as it was downhill for quite a piece, the good Captain experienced a thrill that he had no liking for and could have wished he had kept his mouth shut.

"Oh, do not tremble, brave Cousin," admonished Phoebe. "It is not as breakneck as it seems. At least, I have not broken *my* neck on it yet. I think it will put you more at ease, with me in the driver's seat, once you have become familiar with my expertise with this vehicle."

Sir Brent had a retort hot upon his tongue but swallowed it with a gulp as the little gig took the turn into the park as smartly as it could and still keep both of its wheels on the ground.

Phoebe drew the little carriage to a stop at an overlook and turned to her passenger.

"There!" she said with a smile. "I'll wager you would not have done it better."

The captain breathed a sigh of relief and replied: "It is not a wager I have any wish to take. You make your point well, I must say."

"I shall take that for an apology and thank you."

"You will hear no objection from me—but I hope you will believe that I harbor no doubt of your skill with the leathers and beg you will refrain from any further demonstrations."

"Is it not a lovely view?" she asked, to change the subject.

"Yes, indeed it is!" he exclaimed, pointedly staring at her.

"Oh really, I thought that such a trite compliment would be beneath you, Brent."

144

"Oh well, I could say your eyes are all the scene I could wish."

"That is even worse! What color are they? Quickly now! No, that is not fair of you!" she cried as he bent to look into them, and she pushed him away. "So much for your compliments, Cousin!"

He laughed. "I will admit that I am no hand at compliments, but that is not to say they are not sincerely meant—but enough of this foolery! There is much that we have to discuss of a more serious nature."

"Well, I do declare! That must make of your compliments something less than serious. I take issue with you, Cousin, then that they are sincerely meant! You are no hand with a compliment in any way at all, and I, too, do suggest that we talk of something more serious. One may hope that you can, but one can never expect it to be particularly *flattering* a topic."

Brent gave her a pained look. "You make me sorry I even tried. Very well, I shall not try flattery with you ever again, since you obviously take it with very poor grace."

A very stubborn look came into Brent's face, and he sat erect, folding his arms very high upon his chest as though he were riding a caisson at parade.

Phoebe stared at him, a faint smile upon her lips, but she offered no reply.

When she did not stir or say a word for some moments, Brent unbent for a fraction of a second to peek at her. She burst into laughter.

"Blast you, Phoebe!" he exclaimed, laughing. "You have ruined a perfectly good pet! I thought sure to make you apologize."

"For what?" she asked, all innocence.

He scratched his head. "Come to think of it, I do

not know! I was sure you had made a fool of me—and now I feel just as foolish for being confused. Dammit all! Do you always make a hash of a fellow when he is trying to be nice to you?"

"Oh well, in that case I do apologize, Cousin! I did not know that that was what you were *trying* to do!"

He held up his hand. "Peace!" he cried. "You have got me on the spit and will not cease until you have done me to a turn—but I do protest I do not deserve it. I come to you full of flattery and with a plan to extricate you from our beloved uncle's clutches, and all the thanks I get is one set down after another. Very well, if you have no wish for me to be your confederate, let us be on our way to Richmond—for I can see that we have got nothing to discuss."

"Oh, I do beg your pardon, Cousin," said Phoebe with an appealing smile. "I had not meant to go so far with you. It is just that I am ever so sharp these days. One cannot deal with his Grace to any effect unless one can give him as good as one is bound to get from him."

She leant over and planted a kiss upon his cheek. "There! That is my poor attempt at making amends."

He smiled. "Ah, now that takes me back to France. It was the way the French officers did, you know, saluting each other with a kiss upon an occasion. Never could get used to the idea then, but methinks it an excellent way to make peace between us cousins. I would return the compliment," and he reached for her.

She drew away from him even as she put out a hand to fend him off.

"I will take the intent for the deed, Cousin! I pray you will not misunderstand my gesture."

He nodded. "Very well, but I do not think it at all

146

fair of you. In France it is tit for tat between the officers. I would have my turn."

"Cousin, I am no French officer, nor are you, nor are we either of us in France at this moment. We are seated in our carriage upon Richmond Hill for the sole purpose of discussing how I may be relieved of the burden of my post. If that is not your purpose, I bid you know it is mine!" she retorted sharply.

"All right, Phoebe, it is down to cases. I promise to behave. The thing of it is, you have got yourself into a very difficult position, my girl."

"Well, don't I know that? If that is your conclusion, we are wasting our time—"

"I pray you will give me my chance to speak, Cousin. As I was saying, it is a most difficult position, but not hopeless. I say difficult because his Grace has what must be what goes for a fondness with him, and it is all for you. He speaks most highly of you—not, you will understand, as any sort of person, but as his housekeeper. I had a chat with him last night before retiring, and he impressed me with his good opinion of you; but I had the distinct feeling it was more pride of possession than anything more flattering. In short, he thinks he has got a good thing in you, and the fact that you are family goes a long way with him."

Phoebe sighed with impatience. "But, Brent, that is not at all to the point! I know all that! That is what makes it all so hopeless!"

"Well, it appears to me that you have only yourself to blame," he retorted. "Obviously, you went far out of your way to win his affection, if he is even capable of so fine a feeling, so I do not see what is so bad—"

She reached for the reins, remarking petulantly:

"Oh, you are no help at all! I never did any such thing, but you will never believe it. We had best—"

He stayed her hand. "Phoebe, I will believe anything you say to me, but you have not said anything but that you are marvelously discontented because you cannot be married out of Pickering Hall, a non sequitur if I ever heard one."

She gave him a withering look. "You are making me out a complaining female."

"Well, that you are and on both counts. The question that is in my mind, especially after his Grace spoke so highly of your service to him, is what exactly do you have to complain about? Obviously he is no taskmaster to you."

"I will ask you one question, Brent. If Uncle Janus was a general over you, how would *you* like it?"

"Ah yes, put it on those terms and I do begin to see what it is. But why, then, did you allow him to become so impressed with you in the first place."

"I swear to you I worked to give him the worst idea of me—but, alas, I only succeeded in trapping myself. You see, Uncle Janus had all his grandnieces out for the purpose of selecting from amongst us a successor to Aunt Sophia—"

"And you won the contest hands down! Was he so charming that you were encouraged to put forth your best efforts?"

"I do not like you, Cousin Maitland. I do not see that we have anything to discuss—"

"Now, Phoebe, I am merely trying to get to the bottom of your discontent. I still do not see what it was that changed your mind. I cannot believe Uncle Janus could charm a babe, not that he would ever try—"

"Well, if you will give me leave to speak and cease

148

your jumping to the wildest conclusions, perhaps your feeble wit will come to an understanding of my situation," she exclaimed angrily.

There was such iciness in her tone that Brent raised his hands to his mouth and looked at her in mock humility. He then gestured with his hand for her to continue, keeping his other hand as a muffle on his lips.

Highly indignant, Phoebe then went on to explain exactly how her very best efforts to convince his Grace not to look in her direction for his housekeeper had served only to draw his attention to her and, ultimately, his approval. "—And so there it was! I had outsmarted myself. To think if I had just been satisfied to go about as quiet as a mouse, his Grace's eye would never have fallen upon me. It only adds so much more bitterness to my cup!"

"Hang me, but that was deucedly clever of you!—but of course, it was deucedly clever of the duke to have seen through your little scheme, too! Dash it all, I'd never have given the old boy that much credit!"

"Well, if I was so deucedly clever, by your lights, and Uncle Janus is so deucedly clever, by your lights, pray exactly where does that leave me—or you, for that matter?"

Brent scratched his head. "Nowhere in particular at the moment, I should say. My idea will not wash in such company, I am thinking."

"What idea was that?"

"Well, I thought it would be the simplest thing for you to run a few tricks upon the old man—but you have already done as much and see where it has gotten you!"

"Brent, you are turning out to be no help at all! For a moment I was thinking that I should be beholden to

149

you for helping me out of my fix, but that was foolish of me. After all, you are not in any good odor with Uncle Janus yourself. So how you could be of the least help to me—"

"Now, you just hold on, Phoebe! I said all was not hopeless, and I meant it. You will see. I am a match for his Grace any day of the week. I just need a little time to think. You know you have not been of the slightest help to yourself in this business, and then, too, I had no idea his Grace was so shrewd a person! I have to revise my estimate of the situation before I can determine a proper course of action for you."

Phoebe reached for the reins again. "Well, do not rush yourself, Cousin! You have my entire lifetime to work out your course of action—"

"No, no! Have a little patience, won't you! I am no mean lad when it comes to strategy, I'll have you know. After all, I have had plenty of practice these past few years, God knows!"

"For heaven's sake, Brent, it is not the Grand Army of Napoleon you have to contend with. It is just a crabby old uncle, I assure you—"

"You can spare me the irony, my dear—but I would point out to you that we have, the both of us, made the worst mistake that one can in planning a campaign. We have gone and underestimated the foe. You upon your first coming and myself just now. I would go carefully. Uncle Janus is obviously no bee-brain, and so we must proceed with caution. We have got to do more than match him in the wit department, especially as he has all the reserves and we have none."

"As far as I am concerned, that is just so much army talk! I do not see that it has any application to the case. Uncle Janus is not an army, I am trying to tell you!"

"I never said he was! But he is opposing you, and therefore he is the foe we have got to get around, nothing more. I am not saying that we have to out-flank him and press home the attack—"

"There you go again!" complained Phoebe. "You sound perfectly nonsensical to me—"

"Ah, I have got it! I see the way to do his business for him—"

"Not murder!" cried Phoebe, horrified.

"Well, of course not!" shouted Brent, quite exasper-ated. "Will you just stop and listen to me! Now, who is jumping to the wildest conclusions?"

"Well, you said to do his business—"

"Oh, Lord love you! It was just a manner of speak-ing! All I mean to say is that I do believe I have found a way for you to get what you wish!"

"I can just imagine the sort of thing you would sug-gest! Do you expect me to threaten and to menace my uncle?"

Brent gave her a look of exasperation. "Cousin, you may rest easy. I assure you I can be more subtle than that! What I have in mind is simply this: You have got to demonstrate to his Grace how very unfit you are for the situation of housekeeper—"

"But I just told you that that is what I tried to do from the first!"

"And it was well done of you, too; but since then you have performed your duties as though you were born to it. Don't you see? Each day that passes and his Grace has nothing truly to complain of in you only adds to the excellent impression you have made with him. You have got to cease being so competent,

151

my dear, give the old boy something to really chew on. Make mistakes—"

"And you call that subtle? Why, he will see in a flash what I am up to! You still sadly underestimate the foe, Captain."

"Oh, I do not suggest that all at once everything goes wrong back the Hall. Start slowly and start small. Little things that you forget to see to. Misunderstanding his wishes in a small way—you know what I mean—and be quite contrite over your lapses. If I know my man, and I am sure that I do, he will be quite forgiving at first, but, ultimately, his patience will be exhausted and his better nature will come to the fore and you will be sent home. The beauty of the scheme is that he will come to believe that the position is just beyond your capability and will harbor no more ill will against you than he has for our other cousins."

"It does not sound an easy scheme. Uncle Janus has proven himself to be quite up to snuff—of course, he will not be expecting me to try anything of the sort, for he must be sure he has completely discouraged me upon that score. That in itself is bound to put him off his guard—and if I do the business ever so carefully—as you say, I must be quite contrite and promise each time to better—yes, tears will not be wasted in this effort. Oh, but I shall have to be so very careful! One misstep and he might very well send me packing, declaring vengeance upon me and my family. It is a great risk!"

"Never fear, Phoebe," encouraged Brent. "You can do it easily, and I shall be around to put in a word to help the business along. Believe me, I can be just as subtle as is needed. It will not fail. I'll give you odds on it."

Chapter XIII

IT BEGAN two days later.

The duke rang for the butler and was annoyed when Addington failed to make an appearance after some five minutes. He rang again and began to fume as the minutes passed and still no butler answered his summons.

He started for the door to investigate what had become of his senior servant, when a discreet knock was heard and Addington came into the room.

"You rang, your Grace?"

"Twice, blast you! Where have you been and what is all that filth upon your clothes, and in your hair? Where the devil have you been, man? Rolling about amongst the cobwebs in the wine cellar or I miss my guess! Addington, if you have been at my stock—"

"I beg your pardon, your Grace, but it was at Miss Phoebe's behest that—"

"You *have* been in the wine cellar, by God!"

"Yes, your Grace. You see, sir, Miss Phoebe insisted that—"

"You have been at the wine—and so early in the day! Never tell me that Miss Phoebe ordered you to indulge—"

"Your Grace, she did not—"

"And to make your appearance before me in such a distressed condition—cobwebs up to the eyebrows, nay, in your very hair! Why, man, you are disguised—and on my best bottles, no doubt!"

"Your Grace, I would explain—"

"Explain all you wish, but not before I discharge you which I do now upon the spot! A bosky butler is the least thing I need!"

"May I speak now, your Grace?" requested Addington, all patience.

"I do not see the need. I do not recall that anything a condemned man had to say ever saved him from the rope."

"Your Grace, Miss Phoebe requested me to order up a cleaning party. She said the condition of the wine cellar was particularly disgraceful—"

"Good God, man! You did not let her—" Speech failed the duke as he stared wide-eyed at the butler.

"It is hardly in my province to tell Miss Phoebe. I did suggest that she not disturb the bottles. I could hardly take it upon myself to say more."

"Why, rot me! The place hasn't been touched since the Hall was built—and there is some rare vintage down there that has lain undisturbed for almost as long as I have been alive! Doesn't she know that?"

"I gathered that she does not, your Grace—er, as a matter of fact, I was not aware of it myself. Where is it kept?"

"Well, of course you would not know! I keep it in a special vault behind—Here now! That is none of your business! But, damme, she is just the one to find it, and if those bottles be disturbed, it will take another lifetime, I swear, for it to settle. I order you to descend at once and stop this crazy business! Send

Miss Phoebe to me! Sophia would never have done anything so brainless! Unless she asked me first!"

Phoebe, appearing very calm and very dusty, came strolling into the reading room.

She smiled at her uncle and greeted him cordially.

He sat staring at her. Finally he raised an accusing finger and pointed it at her. "You are a disgrace! Since when does the Mistress of Pickering Hall roll about in the dust with her servants! I demand to know exactly what has been going on down there!"

"I do not see what there is to call forth such agitation in you, Uncle. I am merely seeing to it that the wine cellar is being put into a condition that will permit one to go about in it without becoming a walking dust heap. Observe, your Grace!" And she spread her skirts with a flick, sending a cloud into the air.

"Aargh! Did you have to do that!" he exclaimed and went off into a fit of coughing.

"Oh, I do beg your pardon, Uncle! I had not thought it was all that bad! Heavens! I was only too right to begin to clean up the cellar!"

"The devil you were! Why could you not have let it lie? It has been undisturbed since my father's time! And, besides, wine is best when it reposes quietly. You are not only stirring up the house, you are stirring up the precious wines! Why did you not come to me? I would have forbidden this undertaking!"

"Truly, Uncle Janus, the wine will not be the worse for lying in clean surroundings. I am sure, given a little time, it will settle down and be just like new."

"I don't want it just like new! Old wine is rare wine, and the older a thing is the better off it is if it be allowed to remain undisturbed."

"Well, that is why I could wish you would not fly up into the boughs so, Uncle Janus. I have no wish to disturb you, and that is why I did not think it at all necessary to bother you with such a trifle. And you have had the disturbance all for nothing in any case, for we have finished, and the cellar is now a joy to behold. The cobwebs are gone, and the bottles are all agleam in the lamplight. You must come down and inspect it."

The duke threw up his hands and groaned. "I assure you, my dear, that cellar will not be a joy to drink from for months at the very least. As to inspecting the damage you have done, I'd sooner go over the ruins of the Hall after it had burned down than to witness my precious vintages so badly manhandled. Go, get out of my sight! Get yourself cleaned up so that I am not reminded of this calamity that you have brought down upon me. There is one consolation—and a poor one at that—but you will never have another excuse to clean up the wine cellar in my lifetime, so this can never happen again."

"I am dreadfully sorry you are taking it so hard, Uncle."

"Well, you could not know, I suppose; but where was Addington? He knows how the wines are to be managed."

"Well, he did say something, but I did not think that anything could be so bad as all the dirt and filth. I did not mean to upset you so."

"I know, I know. Next time pay heed to Addington. For now, I will overlook it."

"You are too kind, Uncle Janus."

She left him shaking his head and muttering under his breath. She was quite pleased with herself. It was a good beginning.

Once out of his Grace's presence, Phoebe betook herself quickly to her cousin. She found him out by the paddock, watching as the grooms put two hunters through their paces.

"Ah, there you are, my little housekeeper!" he exclaimed upon catching sight of her. "How goes it?"

"Very well indeed! I have just managed to ruin his Grace's cellar for a time, and he has had to swallow it. He did not like it one bit, but he put a reasonably good face upon it."

Brent winced. "Oh, that was a particularly nasty business! How did you manage it?"

With much impish glee, she regaled her cousin with her exploit and how it was received by the duke.

Brent shook his head. "He's taken it a good deal better than *I* should have. Had I been his Grace, I'd have sent you and Addington packing in a minute!"

"Well, I told you Uncle Janus is not at all an easy man to predict—but I think I have got him off to a good start. Now, what shall I serve him for an encore? Do you have any ideas?"

Brent leaned up against the fence. "I fear I must leave the tactics of this campaign up to you, my dear. You are more bloody-minded than I could ever be— Egad! To ruin a man's wine store! I do not envy my uncle his next course you will serve him."

"You make me sound a positive villainess!" she retorted stormily.

"Well, my dear, you are no heroine in this piece. Can you not find something easier for the old man to have to stomach?"

"Very well, if you do not like my methods, then you should come up with one of your own. Just remember, Uncle Janus is no fool, and it has got to be

157

exquisitely subtle. If it looks in the least contrived, he will find me out in a flash."

Brent wrinkled his forehead in thought for a moment and finally shook his head. "How can I think of anything? What do I know of managing a great household? If it were some commander that I had a wish to discomfit, it would be child's play for me, but, in this, you are the expert. I say do your damndest and the best you know how, whatever the cost to his Grace!"

"Oh, that is so easy to say but it is no help at all, Cousin! Why must I have to do everything?"

"Well, for goodness sake, Phoebe, it is you who have the wish to get out of it! I should think then that it must be up to you to get it done. All I promised was to lay out the strategy for you. If I could do more, I should—but I have got to watch my step around the old man, too, don't you know. I expect we shall be hearing one day soon from Bow Street, and I'd not want his Grace to be on the outs with me just at the moment they make their call. I have never been in a sponging house yet, and I have no wish to enjoy that sort of hospitality even now. Pickering Hall suits me down to the ground."

"I am sorry, Brent, I was not thinking. I guess we all have our troubles, and I shall just have to go it alone—but, if you should happen to get any ideas, do not hesitate to let me know."

That night, as she lay in her bed trying to compose herself for sleep, Phoebe gave thought to her problem. It was not easy to think of another bit of annoyance for her uncle's benefit, especially as he knew what she was capable of cooking up.

And Brent had proved no help at all. He had not

seemed the least bit enthusiastic when he had related to him how well she had gotten started with Uncle Janus. Perhaps to him it was just a game, and, as he could have no great hand in it, his interest flagged.

Well, enough of Brent. She had her work cut out for her. What could she do next? Oh, there were all sorts of tricks and manoeuvers ready to her hand, but they were all of them too obvious. She had to find something that might puzzle his Grace, yet leave him in the belief that it was truly a matter of incompetence with her and not premeditation. It could be nothing like the schemes she had worked, making of her cousins her tools. She had only the servants to work with—and she must be wary of Addington. She had a suspicion the butler was up to all the dodges, too, and could never be trusted not to give the game away—but just a moment! Would he not be the perfect foil if she could drag him into the game somehow?

She thought about that for a moment and then dismissed it. Addington would only get into trouble with the duke, and that she had no wish to see. She had better go to work with those of her people who could not be blamed for carrying out the orders they were given. Yes, that was it! Somehow she must bring them all into it so that both her uncle and Addington would be forced to believe that Pickering Hall was just too much for her to manage. That, of course, was exactly what she wished.

Tomorrow she would study to be a bit confusing in her instructions to the staff, just enough to cause a mild confusion, and, when it was brought back to her, she would be *so* distressed and plead a poor memory—and proceed to do the business all over again. It would not be something to accomplish in a day or a week. It must take time, time for the duke to grow more and more uncomfortable until his patience ran out. Up to now she had done her work too well, and his Grace had never a reason to be in the least way dissatisfied—that is, not until this morning with the wine cellar—and so she had to undo all that good opinion he had of her. Too bad she had given up hope so quickly. If she had not taken up Pickering Hall so easily, any laspes in her good judgement would have been a lot easier to explain. Oh well, she had no regrets. Mistress of Pickering Hall was not all that bad—if only it was for a different Grade. Now, if it had been Brent who had been Grade—

What exasperated Phoebe most in the days that followed was not his Grace's complaints at the way the service was going to pieces, for that was quite what she had hoped for; no, it was Brent's complete lack of sympathy. Surely he could be expected to understand that, if the duke's comfort was being toyed with, his comfort, too, must also suffer. How would it look if Brent's linen came back from the laundresses in perfect condition while the duke's showed signs of less than perfect mangling? She tried to explain to him how it was, and, although he accepted the necessity of it all right, he was not happy about it.

Day followed day, and the duke's complaints grew apace. He began to call Phoebe to account and demand that she pay closer attention to what was going on. He demanded that she discharge any of the help who were proving themselves not up to snuff. He pointed out to her that he, Grade, was becoming ashamed of Pickering Hall and that there was no excuse for it.

She, very apologetic, promised to try harder and

swore there would be no repetition of these blunders on her part, leaving the old man fuming and exasperated.

The day finally came where there was no butter on the table for his Grace's bread. He went up like a rocket and began to dress Addington down. Phoebe intervened to take the blame upon herself. She explained that she had forgotten to put it down on her list the day before.

His Grace, filled with rage, was not to be put off his victim. He shouted: "Then Addington should have seen to it the lack was remedied! He is the butler, and it is his responsibility to see to it that there is butter for my bread!"

"But, Uncle Janus, he had every reason to believe that I had seen to the provisions. After all, I had told him I should!"

"But you had forgotten! He should have gone right back to town and procured it—or sent someone for it! What have I got a great staff of servants for if I am not to have butter for my bread?"

"Truly, Uncle Janus, it comes back to me. It was my duty to see that everything was in order. You cannot expect the butler to catechize the mistress of the house."

"I can and I do! I'll get me a butler who will see to everything, including the mistress of the house! Addington, you are sacked!"

Phoebe thought that now was the time. "Uncle Janus, much as it grieves me to say it, if anyone is to get the sack, it should be myself," and she let a teardrop roll down her cheek to give authenticity to her distress.

"Yes, my dear, I quite agree"—Phoebe's heart leaped—"but, as I cannot sack you, I'll sack Addington!

Now, you, fellow, go into town or to the nearest farm and bring me back butter for my bread, hear?"

Addington scurried out.

Brent was laughing.

His Grace turned to him. "So, Nephew, you find amusement in it, do you?"

"Aye, Great-uncle, I do. All this for a few measly pats of butter?"

"No, my boy, there is more involved in this than a few measly pats of butter. The Hall appears to have come upon hard times when no one, not even its mistress, can carry out the simplest tasks. It was never like this when your Aunt Sophia was about! Never thought I should come to miss the old girl so much. Such a thing was unheard-of in her time!"

"Then it appears to me that what you need is another Aunt Sophia, your Grace. Obviously, you are overburdening poor, dear Cousin Phoebe. So it appears to me."

"I deeply appreciate your opinion, Nephew, and will give it all the consideration it deserves," the duke retorted sourly. He turned to Phoebe: "Now, young lady, I will have you understand this one thing: No matter how you think to flummox me, you'll get no change out of me. I am onto your game, and, if you insist, we shall play at it forever. Pickering Hall is your home, and I have your parents' consent to it— Aye, even their gratitude! So, if it amuses you to see your dear old uncle put to the discomforts of Job, go to it, for like Job, I have the patience of a saint and will see you a properly behaved lady before I am done!"

He threw down his napkin, snatched up his walking stick, leaning heavily upon it as he limped out of the room.

Phoebe remained sitting at the table, her head hanging over her hands clasped upon the cloth.

"I am dreadfully sorry, Cousin," said Brent, looking at her, his lips pressed tightly together.

Phoebe did not look at him. She did not stir.

"Well now, that is not the truth! The fact of the matter is that I am relieved it did not work, my dear. Happy, in fact."

She looked up at him then, a pained and bewildered expression on her face.

He arose from his seat and came over to her.

"Cousin, I pray you will not look at me in that way. I never betrayed you. You saw how I, thinking that this was the time to make what little contribution to the cause that I could, tried to push his Grace in the direction you wished. But he would not have it and so I am glad—for my heart was not in it."

"I—I do not understand you, Cousin! You it was who suggested this course to me. Now you say you regretted it?"

"Aye, and very soon after, for it came to me that if you did succeed with his Grace, I should lose you—and I never wanted that!"

He was smiling at her and shaking his head. "Truly, Cousin, it is not his Grace that has kept me here."

Phoebe was suddenly all atremble within with a great happiness, but she could not believe her ears. "I do not know what to make of you, Cousin. You have no money and are here because his Grace allows it."

He raised her hand to his lips and gently kissed it. "Nonsense, my sweet. Uncle Janus has not money enough to keep me at his side. I came to him only to see if he would give me anything to make my travels more comfortable. Obviously I could not stay on in England, my prospects being what they are—but

163

when I saw you, I changed my mind. Now I am quite content to await the succession, and I care not how long it takes just so long as we can be together. But you say nothing, Cousin! Did returning to Stevenage mean so much to you?"

She arose from the table, beaming: "It does not mean anything at all to me now, Cousin!" and suddenly she was deep within his arms, her lips pressed up to his. It was breathtaking, it was different. She had been kissed before, but it had never been like this! She had never thought it could be so wonderful, and, for her, time stood still for this glorious moment. She loved Brent! And, wonder of wonders, he loved her! How utterly perfect the world and all was become!

"Dearest, sweetest of cousins," murmured Brent. "Oh, how I have been longing for this moment!"

Phoebe leaned back in his arms and looked up into his face. He was smiling down upon her.

"My love, it will not be easy for us. Uncle Janus must never know."

She frowned. "Why not? Surely he could not object to our getting married."

"Do you think he will jump for joy to hear the news? I think not. I think he will go all out to separate us. He has no wish to lose his housekeeper—and surely he must if we are wed."

"But that is nonsense, Brent! We can stay on here at the Hall. There is plenty of room, and I can still see to his comfort. I think it would be a most convenient arrangement."

He broke loose from her. "You know how little love he has for me! He would never put up with me as a permanent sort of guest in his house. He is only tolerating my presence, and even now, I daresay, he regrets ever having allowed me to stay. You know what he is! You are not here because he has any avuncular affection for you! You are his housekeeper, and, if you were to wed me, he could hardly treat with you as meanly as before. For one thing, *I* should not stand for it! No, I tell you we had better keep it from him for a time—at least until the runners from Bow Street track me down. If his Grace will settle my accounts, then it will be time to make plans. At least my credit with the London merchants will have been restored."

"But of what avail is that? We should have no money and have to live on tick with the result that we shall be forced to come crawling back here on our knees to Uncle Janus. Oh, he will think it one grand joke!"

Brent knitted his brows. He sighed heavily. "Phoebe, love, we are not going to settle our future this very moment, and we may be assured it will not be tomorrow either. We have got to think, and, in the meantime, who knows how things may change for us. I say that we keep this happiness to ourselves, at least until we see what Uncle Janus will do about my debts. If he refuses his aid to me, then we must part. I cannot stay on with you and know that I may never have you for my own. I shall have to go forth and somehow, by hook or by crook, find the wherewithal sufficient to an independence. Then and only then can I come back for you."

"But Brent, we have only just declared ourselves, and here you are talking of parting! You make my head spin with doubt of the depth of your love!"

"Oh, never doubt it, sweetheart, not for a moment! I have fallen more deeply in love with you with each passing day, each passing minute! Never fear, we shall have our moments together! But for how long it

165

can go on depends upon fate and his Grace. That is all I wish to point out to you, my love."

"Well, I should think you could have found a better time for it than this particular moment," she declared, pouting.

Brent laughed and drew her close to him again.

"Er—ahem!" said Addington, coming in to the dining room. "Er—Miss Phoebe, if dinner is over, I shall have the table cleared."

They had sprung apart and were now looking as nonchalant as was possible under the circumstances.

"Of course, Addington," said Phoebe, taking Brent's arm and sauntering out of the room with him.

Chapter XIV

PEACE DESCENDED upon Pickering Hall, Phoebe took up the reins of the household, and the duke was satisfied to continue in his comfortable way of carping and criticizing everyone he came into contact with. He made no reference to Phoebe's recent fall from grace, and, with her, he was mild—by comparison with his attitude to the rest of the menage.

In particular, he found fault with Brent, constantly growling the complaint that a fellow so hearty and so well before the world must be good for something, although for the life of his Grace he did not know what.

Brent was not up to his usual humor and refrained from responding to his uncle's taunts, and the duke averred that his lack of response could only signal the fact that Brent was in agreement.

"A fine thing that is!" declared his Grace. "I have got me a nephew who is good for nothing, and he knows it. Well, it is some consolation, for I venture to say there are innumerable heirs who share that same state but they will never admit it. I have an honest heir. Now, will someone pray instruct me as to how that is any advantage to me?"

Of course, there was no answer to his request. Brent and Phoebe could only exchange glances helplessly before the old man, restraining themselves until they could be alone together and pour out their hurts and sympathy, giving to each other what comfort they could.

Brent took to riding out on the estate to avoid being in his Grace's company, and Phoebe, after having seen to it that the household was in order for the day, would ride out after him, bearing a picnic luncheon so that they need not return to the Hall until dinnertime. His Grace did not seem to mind. In fact, he went on as was his wont, having his cronies in, reading his newspaper, and taking the air out on the lawn. If he missed Phoebe's company, he never brought the matter up.

It went on like this for a number of days, the more at ease the duke appeared to be, the more distraught grew Phoebe and Brent.

"Damn!" exclaimed Brent one day as they strolled through a small wood on the estate leading their horses. "There was a time that I wished I could disappear forever from the notice of my creditors! Now, I cannot wait for them to come up with me so that we will know at last what his Grace intends."

"Brent dearest, why do you not go to Uncle Janus and request from him a statement of his intentions. He has pretty well indicated that he will cover your debts, and it is only a matter of what income he will settle upon you now. Perhaps we might even tell him of our love, and that will tilt the balance."

"Oh, aye, it will tilt the balance, I am sure!" scorned Brent. "It will capsize the scales, and we shall never have a chance at happiness. No, that is a poor idea, knowing his Grace. Nor can I see that I will gain any advantage if I were to come right out and ask him. You hear how he digs at me as a worthless idler every chance he gets. How can I request an independence from him when he is all disapproval of me? No, it is better to await events so that I do not appear a beggar in his eyes as well. Be patient, my love, it cannot be for much longer. My creditors are not patient men."

But Phoebe was just as impatient as Brent's creditors, if not more so. Since Brent was not about to make a move until he understood Uncle Janus's intentions, she was not content to sit about idly with him. They had got to make their plans. There was no assurance that Uncle Janus, when faced with the business, would do as he had said, and, certainly, there was even less of an assurance that his Grace would go further and grant to his heir an independence. In fact, she was come to believe with Brent that Uncle Janus might actively resent his housekeeper running off with his heir. Of course, putting it that way, it sounded so much worse than it was. They were, all of them, Harewoods, and, if not upon the same social level, Brent and she certainly were, especially as neither the one nor the other had a penny to their names.

And there was the rub! What plans could they make? Elope? That would not put a farthing into their pockets, and, as Brent had not even the sense to go on half-pay status with the military until he knew what was what, they would have not a feather to fly with, literally. Oh, it was not fair of her to cast any aspersions upon Brent for his lapse! How was he to know that the love of his life awaited him at Pickering Hall? Nevertheless, something had to be planned in the eventuality that Uncle Janus was adamant in his refusal to help. But what? She wondered if she might apply to her uncle for a stipend in payment for her services, just as though she were truly a housekeeper hired out to him. No, she could never ask that! It was too demeaning—and in any case she could see with what humor his Grace would receive such impertinence. No, he would not send her away, worse luck! He would just glare at her and give her a lecture upon poor relations who did not know their place. She could do without that!

As Brent had promised, the waiting was not easy. She was not at all as sanguine as he about his chances of gaining support from Uncle Janus, and that made the waiting all the more bitter for her. Whenever the creditors should finally descend upon Brent, it was just as likely that Uncle Janus would send him packing as not. And, if Brent were no longer permitted the freedom of Pickering Hall and had to leave, where would he choose to go—and what would become of her? Oh dear, what an odious business it was to fall in love with a relation as poor as oneself!

When Phoebe and Brent had come to think that the business of his debts was a long way in the future to being settled, and they had been able to put it out of their minds and enjoy each other's company, the matter was suddenly thrust upon them with consequences that neither of them had foreseen.

It was late one morning that Addington came to Phoebe and presented her with a card. Wondering who could be calling at Pickering Hall so early in the day, she took it from the butler and read the name.

"You say this person has a wish to call upon his Grace? Who is he? I am not acquainted with the name."

"Miss Phoebe, Mr. Travers is his Grace's man of business in London. He has given me to understand

170

that he is expected by his Grace. As I was unaware of his coming, I thought it best to inform you."

Phoebe looked puzzled. "This is the first I have heard of it—or him. Thank you for letting me know. I daresay we had best set another place for lunch as Mr. Travers is bound to be staying. I do wish his Grace would give me notice of something like this. Well, I have naught to say to Mr. Travers. You had best show him directly in to his Grace."

"Very good, Miss Phoebe."

Addington withdrew, and Phoebe returned her attention to the household books of account, which she was in the process of bringing up to date. It was a chore she did not mind overmuch but wished that his Grace kept a steward about the place for just this sort of responsibility. The duke seemed to take an inordinate joy in going over her entries and challenging any he thought in error. She was too careful at it ever to have been caught out and could always defeat his Grace's challenges with valid explanations. He never grumbled at his thrusts being so deftly turned aside but grinned with satisfaction, saying, sooner or later: "Well, my dear, you may never be the housekeeper Sophia was, but I will say this for you, you keep better accounts than she ever could."

She had fallen a little behind and was now in a bit of a rush to bring everything up to date, not for fear of what his Grace might say, but because she hated to be in arrears in anything she did. It can be understood, therefore, if she was a little annoyed to have her efforts interrupted by Addington's coming back into the room to give her a message.

"Yes, Addington, what now?"

"His Grace requires your presence in the library without delay."

171

"Is Mr. Travers with him?"

"Aye, Miss Phoebe—and Sir Brent as well."

"That is odd! I shall go at once."

She hurried out and made her way to the library where she discovered her uncle seated at his writing table with Mr. Travers across from him. Brent was standing to one side of the room, a strained expression on his face.

"Ah, come in, my dear!" called out the duke. "I would have you meet with Mr. Travers, my man of business. Travers, Miss Phoebe Grantham is my grandniece and does me the honor of serving as my hostess."

Mr. Travers, who along with his Grace had arisen upon her entrance, performed a bow and said: "A pleasure to make your acquaintance, Miss Grantham. His Grace, your uncle, has words of the highest praise for you. Please call upon me at any time. I shall be happy to serve you."

"You are very kind, Mr. Travers," she responded and took a chair at her uncle's gesture.

The two gentlemen resumed their seats, and the duke said: "Now then—Maitland!" he interrupted himself to glare at Brent. "Will you not be joining us?"

"Thank you, Uncle, but I prefer to stand. I have a feeling that what is in the wind is not to my comfort."

The duke ignored him and addressed Mr. Travers: "Do you have the papers?"

Mr. Travers reached into a portfolio and brought out a manila envelope which he handed over to his Grace.

"Thank you, Travers. Now if you will be kind enough to wait for us in the drawing room, I shall speak further with you anon."

Mr. Travers looked a bit disconcerted but rose immediately, bowed, and withdrew.

The duke glared at Brent. "For God's sake, do be seated!" he exclaimed. "I do not care to have to crane my neck speaking to you!"

Brent dropped into the seat Mr. Travers had just vacated and said nothing.

"I suppose you have guessed what it is that Travers has brought?"

Brent nodded.

Phoebe said: "I do not understand what this is about."

"My dear, I have commissioned Travers to collect all the accounts your cousin left behind him in London, and that is what he has done—"

"But, Uncle Janus, what business is it of mine? I am sure that what is to follow cannot be at all pleasant for Cousin Brent and must be most embarrassing. I am sure that he cannot wish for my presence upon such an occasion."

The duke turned to Brent: "What say you to that?"

"If Cousin Phoebe's presence will ameliorate the dusting you are about to lay upon me, I beg that she be permitted to stay, your Grace."

"Well, whether your cousin is with us or no, it will make not a tittle of difference in what I have to say to you—but I would have her present because this is a family matter, and, whether I agree with them or not, I shall welcome any comments she has to make about the business."

He stopped and looked at them both for a moment. Neither of them had any response to offer.

The duke began to leaf through the papers quickly. Every now and then he would shake his head and snort. From the sheaf he selected out two sheets and put the rest aside. These he straightened out before him and then paused to regard his little audience once again.

"I do believe I am ready to begin. I have here on the one hand a list of what you owe, Maitland, and it is totalled. If this is complete—Here! Look it over and tell me if it is."

He handed it over to Brent. Brent glanced at the list and turned pale. He looked at his uncle and exclaimed: "Your Grace, I had no idea—"

"No, of course you did not. I believe it was a cow you said? Looks more like the beginning of a herd I should think."

Phoebe, a very troubled look upon her face, inquired: "What does it all come to, Cousin?"

"Thirty-four hundred and twenty-nine pounds, twelve and six," he replied despondently.

"No!" cried Phoebe, shocked to the core.

"Yes, my dear," affirmed his Grace. "See what manner of man is your cousin! Not only is he spendthrift and a waster, but he cannot even keep his accounts straight! Why, for such a sum I am sure they'd hang him but for the fact that he is a Harewood and my heir—"

"Oh, I beg you, Uncle, not to say so!" exclaimed Phoebe in dismay.

"Well, of course we do not hang people for debt no matter how great the sum—but I can assure you that this cousin of yours has bought himself a life ticket to Newgate! Fat chance of him finding any such sum short of my demise."

Very grimly, Brent stared at the old man. "I apologize, Uncle, for not having kept better track of my debts. As you will see, if you care to look, many of them are from before I entered into the service—"

174

"Ran away from, you mean!" declared the duke.

"Be that as it may, I had other things on my mind for a number of years, something more important to England and my own survival than paltry money."

"Will you listen to the fellow! Paltry it is, I dare say, when you have not got it! Wait, my dear fellow, until it is yours, and we shall see how paltry it is!"

"Uncle Janus, what is all this in aid of? Unless you are to intervene, such a tremendous sum leaves me but two alternatives to choose between."

"And they are?"

"I can flee the country—"

Phoebe gasped.

"—or I can go to the sixty percents and let them tell me what my prospects are worth to me. I venture to say they will be worth something more than three or four thousand pounds, don't you think?"

"Yes, well, we shall not have any of that! I know what my responsibilities are, and there is no need to talk of sixty percents or running off to America. I have here a letter of credit for Travers to take back with him to town and settle up these accounts of yours—"

"Oh, that is most kind of you, Uncle Janus!" exclaimed Phoebe in the greatest relief.

"I thank you, Niece, for your approval—but that is not to say that I do not intend to let the account of this wastrel go unpaid, mind you."

"I don't understand, sir," interposed Brent. "Do you mean for me to reimburse you"

"Not me, but the family! This money, being paid out upon your account, is out of the Harewood fortunes, and it shall have to be made good by you."

"By me, sir? I do not see how I—"

"It is quite simple. You shall go to work and see me paid out of the stipend you shall earn."

Brent raised a hand to his puzzled brow. "What the deuce can I work at that will even begin to pay off such a monstrous sum?"

"It so happens that the Harewood seat is in need of a steward. The place is going to wreck and ruin ever since I elected to make my residence here in Richmond. The people I have got out there are all well and good, but it is not as if the estate were their own. You know how that is. You shall go out there and see to it that the property is put into shape and that the tenants are brought into line. You are an officer of the military, and I expect that you can make it pay instead of being the bottomless pit it for Harewood money has become. Whatever you can produce, over and above expenses, will be credited against the thirty-four hundred you owe the Harewoods. Now I think that is eminently fair, don't you?"

"You mean to send me out to Cornwall? Why, that is the end of the world, sir!"

"Beggars cannot be choosers, sir, and you are a beggar, by God!"

Phoebe's heart beat againt her breast as she saw the anger mount up into Brent's face. She did not wish for him to make an open break with her uncle, and yet she never wished that he would accept such an odious ukase from his Grace. In either event she must be the loser, for it spelled Brent's removal from Pickering Hall.

"No, by damn!" shouted Brent. "You'll not send me out to Cornwall, an impoverished hanger-on in exile! If I must leave, it will be for a destination of my own choosing! Good Uncle, do not toy with me! Either sign that damned letter or be done with the business and I'll bid you good day!"

In the violence of his emotion, he had arisen from his chair and was now leaning upon his fist on the top of the writing table, staring defiantly at the old peer.

His Grace was not in the least discomfited. He leaned back in his seat and stared right back at his heir.

"Sit, Maitland, and put a damper on that temper of yours! Now see how provident I was to have Phoebe stay with us. Let us put it to her if my offer is fair or not."

Turning to Phoebe, he asked: "Fair Portia, a judgement, I pray. What think you of Sir Brent, in all duty to his Harewood heritage and inheritance, what say you to his going out to Grade and overseeing his patrimony—well, that is not exactly the term for it, is it, but you know what I mean—What say you, my dear?"

For the moment Phoebe could not find her voice. She could only shake her head. The duke's eyebrows shot up.

"Well, I must say your Aunt Sophia would never have thought to cross me in anything so important as this!" he exclaimed, very displeased. "In any case, I would appreciate a statement from you on the matter, for a mere shake of the head is impossible to debate with, you will admit."

"Your Grace, I have no wish to interfere. I am sure that you must know what is best in the family's interest. It is only that Cousin Brent is but newly returned to us. I could hope that we may have the pleasure of his company for a little longer. Grade in Cornwall has existed despite your absence from it these many years. I am sure it will still be there whenever you and Cousin Brent can manage to come to terms with respect to it."

"Hmmmmmm!" murmured the duke. "It is not the existence of Grade that is in question, young lady, but its rents and income—"

"Your Grace," Brent hastened to say, "I do not see the necessity of my going out there for quite a long while. I have been back from France only a matter of months. There are—er—things I have a wish to do. I am still a young man, yet to be married—"

"Married! Ah, there's a word with a good ring to it!" exclaimed his Grace. "Pray let us examine into it for the moment. Perhaps we can forget Cornwall."

Phoebe wet her lips nervously.

His Grace was continuing. "Yes, marriage may be the perfect answer to your problems, my dear boy."

Brent was eyeing his uncle askance.

"What have I said, Brent, that you should look at me so warily? Do you have something against marriage?"

"No, I have nothing against marriage. In fact, the idea of taking a wife is not at all foreign to my thinking at the moment. The thing is I have naught to offer my lady of choice, you see."

"I see nothing of the sort!" snorted his Grace. "It is never a question of what you have to offer, my boy, but what the lady of your choosing has to offer. Remember she is to become a duchess—in due time, that is," he said with a grimace.

"You would have me barter my prospects for hard cash? Why, that is no better than going to the sixty percents! At least with them I do not have to engage in matrimony!"

Phoebe's heart had almost ceased its beating as she

178

saw what her uncle was driving at. She sat impassively, waiting for him to destroy this newfound happiness of hers. She wished she had been clever enough to have foreseen her uncle's move. She never would have objected to Brent's going out to Cornwall.

"Bah, you prate like a fool!" retorted his Grace. "What a thing to do, to speak of percents and marriage as though there was any comparison!"

"Do you have someone particular in mind for me?" asked Brent.

His Grace shrugged. "I am not particular. The neighborhood is overrun with eligible heiresses. You take your pick. So long as she is rich, I shall have nothing to say against it. My only concern is to see to it that the Harewood treasure which needs must be so sadly depleted in your interest is restored. I'll pay the shot and never ask a penny of you if, by means of matrimony, you bring a good fortune and a good connection to our family."

To Phoebe's dismay, Brent nodded. "It is worth considering. Now, you cannot expect me to go about the business in any great rush. For one thing, I do not know any of the young ladies of the neighborhood—"

"Oh, we can take care of that right quickly. I, Grade, shall give a series of parties and balls and what have you in honor of the return of the Harewood Hero. You'll have an opportunity to meet and measure up every last one of them. You, Phoebe, can have the pleasure of arranging everything. I am sure you will do your cousin proud."

Phoebe swallowed hard. Things were advancing in a far worse fashion than she could have believed. She wished she were a thousand miles away and that this day had never dawned.

"Still, your Grace, it is not a step to be taken in an

instant. I shall have to not only get acquainted with the various females, but their families and their prospects as well. That is bound to take some time."

Phoebe was breathing more easily as she understood what Brent was up to.

"Well, of course it is bound to take some time. Phoebe, how long will you require to complete preparations for a grand ball?"

She was quite prepared for that inquiry and replied without hesitation: "Since it has not been our practice to entertain, Uncle Janus, it must be at least a month before the invitations could be sent out."

"As long as that? Well, I shall expect a bang-up affair, and I suppose you will need some time—"

Brent broke in: "And, as for me, I am sure that I shall be all of three months at—"

"A month to get ready and a month to go!" snapped his Grace. "That is all the time you shall have, and that is all the time you shall need. You are a soldier and know how to mount an effective campaign. It is not as if you have got to get the gel to fall in love with you, you know. Just get married to her so that I may take a hand in the marriage settlements. Two months ought to be quite sufficient, I am sure, so you had better get right to work and make yourself known about the neighborhood before the ball. If you like, we can make the affair a celebration of your engagement to whatever unfortunate your choice happens to descend upon."

"Er—no, Uncle, I'd as soon we did not take our fences before we got to 'em," objected Brent. "A simple affair will be just fine, I am sure."

"Very well, have it any way you wish. Phoebe, see to it and do not spare the expense. After all, we are about to create the next Duchess of Grade, don't you know!"

Neither Phoebe nor Brent looked particularly over-joyed at that glorious bit of news.

Chapter XV

PHOEBE CAME RUNNING to Brent in the garden behind the house, and he caught her to him and held her close.

"Oh, my dear, whatever are we going to do?" cried Phoebe, looking up into Brent's eyes.

As he drew her over to a garden seat, Brent said heavily: "Blast if I know! But it was the best I could do with the old tyrant!"

"The best you could do? Oh, surely it had been better if you had gone out to Cornwall—"

"No, never! I could never leave you, Cousin!"

"Brent, what are you saying?" she cried. "What will it matter if you are married? At least with you away in Cornwall we could have had the hope that somehow, someday. We could make our love known—"

"Oh, but surely, my love, you must realize that is nonsense! Would you have me rusticate amongst the sheep or swine or whatever it is they devote themselves to in Cornwall? Is that a fitting fate for me?"

"But, Brent, can you even think it is better to stay on here under the condition that you prepare for a loveless marriage? I should prefer to have you rusticated than wedded!"

"Phoebe, my love, you are rushing the business! I am not wed yet, and there is plenty of time before—"

183

"But there is no time, don't you understand? You have got to go to Uncle Janus at once and accept the stewardship at Grade—then we shall have time!"

A stubborn frown creased Brent's brow. "That is not my way! I am not defeated yet and have no intention of going down on my knees to his Grace. I shall hold the line and meet the enemy face to face—"

"That is purely nonsense! His Grace is no fool! He'll see to it you are wed. To stay on is to invite the very defeat you disdain, and I shall be slain! Brent, if you love me, go at once to our uncle and accept Cornwall. I beg you!"

"What sort of life will that be for either of us, separated by some two hundred and fifty miles? No, I say!"

"Then you do not truly love me!" she accused him.

His face was cold and stiff. "I may make that charge against you as easily. If you truly loved me, you would not wish to be separated."

"Oh, that is not true! Brent, it is not reasonable that you can expect to stay on at Pickering Hall and not do as his Grace commands."

"There is plenty of time before I have to haul up the white flag. We have all of two months before the shoe begins to pinch."

"Two months? But that is all his Grace has allowed you! Do you think that he will rest easily for all that time, fully content to leave all up to you? He is never so foolish, I tell you! Brent, before it is too late, I insist you go to his Grace and accept Cornwall!"

"You insist, do you? One would think that we were already married and you had a right—"

Phoebe was staring at him horrified. Now her features became as stiff as had been Brent's. Very coolly she said: "No, Brent, you are quite right. I have no

184

rights in the matter at all. How foolish of me to have thought so."

She turned on her heel and marched back into the house.

Brent cried out: "Phoebe, stay! Don't run off—" His voice died away as he stared after her. "Damn!" he swore under his breath. "Captain Maitland, I thought you were smarter than that!"

There was a coolness in the house after that, but his Grace did not appear to notice. As a matter of fact, he was greatly heartened to see his young housekeeper devote herself to the arrangements for the gala occasion with unstinting effort. Many were the occasions that she found to consult with the old gentleman, and she seemed content to receive his suggestions just as he was flattered to have been asked for them. During the weeks that followed, great-uncle and grandniece proceeded along the friendliest of lines, and one had the distinct impression that the both of them were equally concerned to rid the premises of the presence of one Captain Sir Brent Maitland.

For his part, Brent did initially attempt to repair the damaged state of affairs between his cousin and himself—

"I say, Phoebe, can we not talk things over? You have not really given ear to me and what I intend, you know."

"Cousin Maitland, by what right do I come to pass judgement upon your intentions, I who have no rights at all in the business as you have so carefully pointed out—"

"Oh, Phoebe—my love, do not take what I said in a

185

fit of temper so to heart. I did not mean a word of it—"

"You most certainly did," she retorted, "or you would have repaired to his Grace by this time and this odious affair that I am arranging would have been canceled."

"But, dammit, girl, that is not a part of my plan!"

"Sir, I could not care less if it is or is not a part of your plan, for whether you go or stay is not any part of *my* plan! Do as you will, but, from this moment on, know, sir, that my sentiments concerning you and your future march with those of our uncle!"

"That is not fair of you! You are raising the odds against my chances of success!"

"Fiddlesticks, my good man, I am only enhancing your chances of success. I could so easily make of the affair a horrible example, but you may rest assured I shall see to it that everything goes well so that the scion of the Harewoods has naught to be ashamed of as he goes forth to seek his bride."

The look of pain upon his countenance was matched by the tone of his voice as he exclaimed: "Phoebe, you cannot say such a thing and still claim you love me!"

"Precisely. Now, do be a good fellow and cease to bother me. I have so much still to do."

Phoebe's attitude towards him remained civil, but only just so, and it was not at all difficult for Brent to convince himself that he had had a narrow escape. So intransigent a female was never for him! Since he was bound and determined not to surrender to the duke's request that he go off to Grade in Cornwall, and, since now he was quite assured of the fact that nothing remained between his cousin and himself, he might just as well enter into the spirit of the thing, even as Phoebe was doing, and, by heaven, find himself a wife! He was quite ready to settle down; and, with a female well-endowed in all respects, what could be better?

Yes! It would put an end to his having to constantly be at duelling with his uncle. Set up with his wife's money, he had no doubt that he could reenter society in a station appropriate to the heir of Grade—and *she* could see how she liked *that*!

But even as that thought came to him, he felt as though he had received a blow in his stomach. It was not at all what he wished.

His Grace was certainly pleased with the way things had turned out. He discoursed at great length with Phoebe upon the prospects of the Harewoods, now that they could all of them look forward to having a duke and a duchess at their head in the very distant future. He declared that it had been bad of him to have neglected that aspect of life, and that he had not been fair to the family fortune by neglecting to present them with a duchess. Of course it was too late for himself to do anything to remedy the lack, but he was quite happy to have got Maitland so thoroughly in his clutches as to force that inconsequential ne'er-do-well to do the necessary.

Phoebe found such conversations quite distressing and would try to excuse herself from them, but his Grace would not let her withdraw until he had gone over the business with her at least a dozen times to make sure that she understood just how the family must now prosper. He even took pains to assure her that she, too, must directly profit from the event as Brent's new lady must be everlastingly grateful to the female who arranged the affair at which Brent selected her as his bride.

Phoebe was quite sure that such gratitude she could do without, but, of course, she never thought to inform his Grace of her thinking.

As the time drew near for the invitations to be sent out, one could have sworn that it must have been a most dreary and mournful occasion that was approaching to see the expressions upon the face of Phoebe and Brent. On the other hand, to see the high good spirits that lighted up the duke's venerable phiz, one could hardly doubt but that it was a most gladsome day that was nigh.

Finally it was done. All the food and refreshments that could possibly be required had been contracted for and delivery promised. All the decorations were in hand, and workman were busy about the Hall, hammering and hanging. The gardens, by dint of great efforts of the husbandmen, were neat and trim as never before, and even Mother Nature cooperated to the extent of excellent growing weather so that all was green and colorful as befitted formal English gardens in all their beauty at the height of the season. Nothing was left but to send out the invitations—and his Grace was on hand to see that they were sent off on schedule.

Immediately thereafter, he demanded of Phoebe that she take Brent about the neighborhood and see to it that he was made known to all the families, especially those who boasted of eligible daughters.

"Truly, Uncle Janus, you cannot believe that a fellow so much before the world has any need of his cousin to take him by the hand and introduce him about. I will be pleased to let Cousin Maitland do the business of his own. I have every confidence he can manage it successfully."

"One would certainly think so, but I do not trust him at it. He has been sitting about the house, lo! these many days, when he could just as easily have been gallivanting about the Hill, ingratiating himself with all and sundry. No, my dear, I do not trust the fellow. You have got to go along and see to it he puts himself in the best light and gets to know as many of those young ladies whose acquaintances I believe you have already made. After all, it would be a shame and a waste if, at the party, Nephew Brent had to spend all of his time first getting acquainted when he should be devoting himself to picking and choosing. I have some reason to believe that my heir's heart is not in this business, and I intend that he will see it through, willy-nilly. He may glibly speak defiance, but I shall not be put off. He is going to settle down and become a credit to this family, or I shall withdraw my recognition of him for as long as I live. He'll not do very comfortably under that circumstance, I vow."

"Oh, but, Uncle Janus, you cannot mean it! You would only force him to go to the moneylenders—"

"No, for if he crosses me in this, all he will inherit is the title and naught else! I will break the entail without the least compunction and distribute the proceeds amongst the rest of the family. He will gain nothing and his prospects will be nil, nothing upon which a sixty percent would grant him a penny. Ah, but perhaps I should not be telling you all this! You must now believe that it is not in your best interest to see the scoundrel married in accordance with my wishes."

Phoebe eyes opened wide as she protested: "Uncle Janus, what can you be thinking of me? That I should stand idly by and see a young man's prospects

189

destroyed, not to say the heritage of the Harewoods into the bargain, is an absolute impossibility! I am distressed even that you would consider so drastic a remedy and shall do my utmost to see to it that Brent does not fail to meet this obligation you have placed upon him."

"Most nobly said, Niece, but why should you exert yourself in Maitland's behalf? It is only to his benefit and never to yours in the end."

Phoebe swallowed hard before she was able to say: "As you yourself have said, Uncle Janus, it is to the family's benefit that we have a duke and his duchess at our head."

"Good girl! I knew I could count on you, dear Phoebe. It was a very good day, the day I elected to have you come to the Hall!"

Chapter XVI

IT IS quite possible that not since the reign of King Charles I had the neighborhood of Richmond, Hill and all, been so agitated over a forthcoming event. It is quite possible that in the minds of more than a few of the residents, the ball to be given by the Duke of Grade at Pickering Hall quite overshadowed Charles's edict enclosing the park and gardens some two hundred years ago, particularly those individuals who might be described as young, fair, and female.

When it had come time to send out the invitations, Grade himself condescended to do the duty—and he accomplished the task in a style that was awesome, indeed. No matter how much Phoebe would have preferred to have remained behind, nothing would satisfy his Grace but that she accompany them, them being himself and nephew Brent. The great ducal coach was run out—it had not seen the light of day in ages—and it was assembled, complete with a pair of liveried footmen up behind and a pair of outriders up before. The coach was gleaming in the sunshine, its emblazoned panels shrieking the ducal crest to the world. It was a sight to be seen only upon a coronation day, and Phoebe felt embarrassed and out of place to have to take her seat in the great vehicle.

The fact that she was seated next to Brent did not make the ordeal any more bearable.

She wondered why the duke should take it upon himself to deliver the invitations, and in such an ostentatious manner. At the very first call, it all became very clear. The duke was out to make sure that everyone knew of his nephew's achievements against the French, of his nephew's prospects as successor to the title and estates of Grade, and—it took no great discernment to understand—when his Grace was closeted with the master and the mistress of the household, he was also making it very plain that Captain Sir Brent Maitland K. C. B. was in the market for a bride.

The pattern was repeated at every household that they called upon, and, each time it happened, Phoebe winced with embarrassment that the duke could be so shameless in his purpose.

She was furious with Brent. He, instead of being modest and retiring about the business, did not hesitate, before her very eyes, to encourage—well, that is a poor word for it—he blatantly flirted with every eligible female in the house, and some not so eligible, as well!

There was never any doubt that all the invitations would be accepted, and that the ball would be the success of the season and of many seasons to come. So rare had been the occasions that Pickering Hall had been lent to any celebration at all, on that count alone, an invitation from the duke would have been considered priceless. But to add to it the presence of a war hero, one that was particularly young and extremely well graced in figure and manner, not just any old dog of war, well, it can be easily imagined the flutter that prospect caused in the breasts of the distaff side of the entire neighborhood. Need it be added that his Grace's unsubtle emphasizing of Captain Sir Brent Maitland's eligibility—he might just as well have said "availability," thought Phoebe—added to the furor and to the anticipation? It began to take on a Cinderella air, except that Brent needed no fairy godmother, his grand-uncle was more than up to the occasion.

When the triumphal Harewood cortege finally drew up before the portals of Pickering Hall, the great coach contained three very tired people, but each of them was in a humor of his own. His Grace was crowing, all jubilant at the ease with which he had managed to guarantee that the ball would be a most excellent affair, nor did he fail to rejoice in the fact that Brent was as good as wed. He had no end of eligible beauties, and wealthy, to choose from.

Brent, having infuriated Phoebe with his manner before their neighbors, now appeared to go out of his way to exasperate her. He merely sat back and chuckled about it all, remarking to her upon the good points of this one and the remarkable points of that one, notwithstanding the fact the Phoebe, sitting in frosty silence, had not a word to say to him or to the distasteful topic of his conversation.

Phoebe was heartsick. She would have wept but for the fact that she was so angry with both of the men of her family and refused to allow them to see how hurt and offended she was. As she dismounted from the carriage, she was quite sure that she had had more than enough of Captain Maitland and would see to it that the ball was every bit the success the duke would have it to be. The sooner the captain was enabled to take his pick and be married, the sooner the old tranquility would return to Pickering Hall. She certainly could stand some peace and quiet. Why, it seemed that ever since Brent—Captain Maitland had made his appearance, things had been at sixes-and-sevens!

"Ma'mselle Phoebe, I cannot!" declared René, folding his arms across the great barrel of his chest, his jowls aquiver with indignation.

"But, René, you promised!" retorted Phoebe. Oh, what a time for her chef to decide that his artistry was being corrupted!

"Ah, but Ma'mselle, you nevair tell René that it would be chafing dishes! 'Prepare,' you say, 'the great spread fit for the king!' and thees I do—but there is no king, there is no dinnair! There is only buffet! *Sacre-bleu!* For this you need a *chef francais?* Bah, I do not finish! Only for the king I finish!"

Phoebe was beside herself with anxiety. It was but an hour before the guests would begin to arrive, and his Grace had insisted that she take her place beside him to receive them as his hostess. She had still to get dressed, and an hour was hardly time enough, yet she must waste precious minutes of it in argument with her fractious chef because he misunderstood her meaning.

"René, it is all a mistake, don't you see? I never claimed that His Majesty would be coming. I only wished that you would prepare an excellent repast, one that even His Majesty, with all his excellent chefs at his disposal, would have enjoyed. His Grace is very proud of you and would have his neighbors learn how excellent is the cuisine of René, chef to the Duke of Grade!"

René looked disappointed. "That is all?" he asked, hurt.

"Oh, but it is a deal more than that, René. Many of

194

the households in the district boast of French chefs, but none can boast of a René. Come, you must do us proud."

"Ver' well, but I prepare a dinnaire, not a buffet!" He spat the word with a distasteful grimace.

"But you have got to! That is how the food is to be served. It will be quite a crush and a formal dinner is not to be contemplated—"

"In that case, I make san'wiches. You English, all the time you eat san'wiches. I do not waste my art upon buffet!"

Phoebe grabbed for the first thought that came to her mind. "Very well, René, prepare sandwiches. We English can judge a sandwich better than all the world—and I cannot recall any Frenchman, chef or no, who can prepare a sandwich to an Englishman's taste, not even the great René."

René frowned, thinking hard.

He looked up and asked: "But, Ma'mselle, how can you compare san'wiches to the finest cuisine of la France? It is to laugh!"

"Oh, indeed, René, I am sure we shall all laugh at your sandwiches."

"But I beg you, Ma'mselle, a buffet for the fine, the delicate dishes I prepare. To stand up and eat of them is sacrilege! One must be seated, napkin under one's chin—"

"Well, this night, René, no one will have time for that—"

"But how then are they to judge—"

"Oh, we English are quite used to dining standing up—especially at great sociables such as his Grace is sponsoring tonight. It is not anything exceptional, I assure you."

Phoebe held her breath for René was thinking again. Finally he nodded.

"Very well, I do it, but only because you are English. For Frenchmen, nevair! It would be an insult to me and to my art!"

"I quite agree—and when we do have some Frenchmen as guests, we shall have this very same feast served at table so it can be very properly appreciated."

"Ah, Ma'mselle, you understand René!" he cried, all grinning. He unfolded his arms and brandished his great soup spoon as though it were a sword. "Nevair fear! Buffet or no buffet, I shall do you and his Grace proud! It shall be a buffet fit for the king!"

"You are too kind, René. Now, I must rush."

She ran from the kitchen and dashed madly up the stairs. She had not even time to feel relieved that the difficulty had been got over.

"Good evening, your Grace," said Phoebe, coming up to her uncle as he stood waiting to receive his guests.

He did not respond but raised a lorgnette to his eyes, something she had never seen him do before. For that matter, she had never seen his Grace so formally decked out. He was wearing silken knee breeches and hose with his sash of office and the star of his rank displayed upon his chest, the very picture of a duke, even to his manner which, at the moment, was unpleasant.

"Dammit, Phoebe, is that the best thing you could find? That is no proper gown for my niece to be wearing at a grand function!"

"I beg your pardon, your Grace, but it *is* the best thing that I have. For all that I am the Mistress of the

196

Manor, I am, also, your poor relation, which you have been at pains to point out to me more than once in the past."

Immediately the duke was his old self. He chuckled crustily and replied: "Never did I think that that bit of rudeness would come home to me in the form of a rebuff! Well, I am pleased to see you in good spirits, my dear. It will be a good idea for you to go into London—next week, I think—and see to purchasing some decent clothing. It will be my pleasure to escort you."

"Thank you, your Grace. You quite overwhelm me, I assure you, but there is never the necessity. This affair is not like to be repeated."

"And why not, may I ask? It is time the old Hall came to life!"

"But for what occasion?"

"Who knows? Who cares? I do not! Who could have foreseen this occasion? One never knows. There may well be others, and, as my hostess, you have got to look a deal more affluent than you are looking this evening."

"As you wish, your Grace, but I still think it is a waste."

"Be that as it may, where the devil is that confounded cousin of yours?" he demanded testily. "Here it is, almost time, and he has not made an appearance. I have a wish to see how well he has got himself up. I never thought to ask the bottomless rogue how he does for clothing—but, considering the size of his debts that I have had the very questionable pleasure of meeting, I daresay he does well enough."

"Indeed, I do, Uncle Janus," said Brent coming up from behind them. "Do you approve, O! master of my fate?"

197

His Grace wheeled about and glared at him. "Well, I'll not say the money you spent upon your back was not well spent. You look fit to be Grade's heir, Nephew," he admitted begrudgingly.

Phoebe had turned with the duke and stood for a moment transfixed. She had always thought her cousin a very handsome gentleman, but, tonight, he was looking perfectly splendid. She was very unhappy to see him looking so fine.

"Well, Cousin, how do you say? Am I fit company for his Grace?"

"I am sure you will do—"

"I thank you—"

"—as long as his Grace approves," she ended.

Brent looked discomposed. He turned to the duke.

"I will say this much, your Grace: A hostess of mine would be fitted out in far greater style than you deem necessary."

His Grace gave him a disdainful look. "And where would you get the wherewithal to be so generous, I wonder."

Brent laughed. "I suppose I should have said 'if I had it to begin with'—but you do, so why is not my cousin appareled as richly as she should be. She is the niece of a wealthy duke, you know. It sort of makes you out something of a pinchpenny, I should say."

"And I have not the least doubt but what you *would* say so. Well, I pray you will not place the blame for it at my door. Speak to your cousin. She never told me of her needs, and blast me if I know what is what with a female and her clothes!"

Brent turned to Phoebe. "It will be my pleasure, Cousin, to escort you to the city and encourage you to spend Uncle Janus's money."

"Here now, you have your own affairs to attend to!"

198

objected his Grace. "And, besides, I have already spoken for the privilege."

"Then blast you!" exclaimed Brent, laughing.

Phoebe could not make them out. Underneath the insults that they bandied back and forth, she could not detect the least note of rancor, and she wondered that she could find no grounds for the essentially good-humored exchange. She was unable to enter into the spirit of it, and that saddened her even more, the thought that Brent was so very unfeeling about what had been between him and herself.

He turned to her, and she feared that he was going to offer her some bright witticism, and she knew she should fall to weeping if he did. Fortunately, just at that moment, the first guests were announced, and his attention was diverted from her. No wonder! Accompanying Lord and Lady Cogswell was their beautiful daughter, Lady Philomena, a vision no man could resist, especially not Brent! she concluded bitterly to herself.

Chapter XVII

IT WAS all going very well, thought Phoebe. The guests seemed to be enjoying themselves and paid many compliments to his Grace for the tasteful magnificence that greeted their eyes as they stood with him, exchanging salutations and introductions at the entrance to the ballroom. As they mingled about the floor, before the dancing had commenced, and visited the buffet, Chef René presiding, there were more compliments, this time for her for the delicious spread which she, in turn, made sure to pass on to René. He was beaming with pride and pleasure and, during the course of the evening, let her know exactly how many offers he had received from the matrons present for his services if ever he had a mind to leave the duke's service. Of course, he swore eternal devotion to his "*chère ma'mselle*," but Phoebe made a note to speak to his Grace about giving him something extra at the end of the quarter.

As for herself, she was satisfied that all was going so well and that his Grace could have no reason to be dissatisfied with any of the arrangements. Getting it all together had been something of an ordeal for her, especially considering that she had never had to do anything like it before. On top of which she had had her own particular problem to worry about, and it had not helped that her heart was not in it to begin with. At the moment she could be at ease over her duties as hostess and give herself over to that other problem which was the center of attention of a group of chattering and laughing females, signing dance cards at a merry pace.

She would have liked to have joined in, to have gotten at least one dance with her cousin—she had never danced with him and now, probably, never would have the opportunity—but could not bring herself, dressed so poorly as she was, to join the group of expensively clad females. It brought a pang to her heart as she recalled how strained was her father's face when he had been presented with the bill for the gown she was now wearing, and it could not hold a candle to the least of the gowns displayed by others this evening.

Since all was proceeding quite smoothly, she thought to remain in the background and move about, attracting as little notice as possible. Unfortunately for her peace of mind, his Grace had other ideas. The dancing was about to commence when Addington made an appearance at her side with a summons from the duke for her to attend him.

She discovered her uncle, surrounded by most of the lords and many of the ladies of the district, engaged in exchanging views and compliments. Standing beside him was Brent, arm-in-arm with the lady he had chosen to be his partner in the dance. Of course it was Lady Philomena. Phoebe was not surprised.

Upon seeing her approach, the duke broke off the conversation and stepped to her, taking her by the hand and leading her up to the group.

"Ladies and gentlemen, pray give me your attention!" he said loudly, and a hush descended on the room. "I have an announcement to make."

There was a general gathering around.

He reached out and took Phoebe and Brent, each by the hand, and walked with them to the center of the floor.

"Ladies and gentlemen here assembled, I beg leave to present to you in the persons of these, my grand-nephew Sir Brent, and my grandniece Miss Grantham, and myself, the family Harewood. Further, in honor of this occasion, I do formally recognize and confirm Captain Sir Brent Maitland, Knight Commander of the Bath, as my heir and successor and, by your courtesy, declare him Marquis St. Cleer!"

Brent was plainly startled and for a moment could do little more than stare at his uncle. Recovering himself, he said, as he bowed to the duke: "Your Grace, I am overwhelmed."

"Yes, I thought you would be. It should definitely make things easier for you. What do you think, my dear?" he asked of Phoebe.

She was aghast with shocked confusion and could not have responded if her life depended on it. Fortunately, there was a press of well-wishers, and she was thrust aside as the entire assemblage moved in to congratulate the flabbergasted captain.

Considering what Brent's attitude had been to her recently, Phoebe had not faced the full meaning of Brent's refusal to take up the work in Cornwall. Perhaps she had the niggling hope that some way, before it was too late, they would compose their differences and work out a future that would see them together. Now, Uncle Janus had shattered that last hope to smithereens with his declaration. Before, as a poor relation, though heir, Brent was on exactly the same level as she was; but now, as Lord St. Cleer, duly recognized by Grade, even though it was only a title of courtesy, it marked him as though he were Grade's son and at once raised him above the rank of commoner, socially, even if not legally.

The prospect of their ever being more to one another than distant relations was gone. The link of blood, so dilute as to never have been any obstacle to their being wed, was now become little more than a mere claim upon his notice. Upon his affections, it was no claim at all.

She stood off to the side and watched Brent acknowledging the good wishes with never a thought of her in his mind, she was sure. Even his Grace had quite forgot his poor relation as he stood beside Brent and lent his dignity to the occasion.

She glanced over the room and up to the balcony where the leader of the orchestra was watching the milling people below waiting patiently for the commotion to subside so that he and his colleagues could begin the music for the dance, and she thought that things were well enough in hand not to require her presence on the floor. Addington was more than capable to see to things from this point on, and she would not be missed. She started to leave.

"Miss Grantham, may I speak with you?" asked a pretty young lady coming up with her.

Phoebe stopped, and, at once, the girl begged her to be introduced to Lord St. Cleer. Phoebe recognized her as Lady Clarinda, a neighbor who had not been about of late, having been off on a prolonged visit to distant relatives. Phoebe suspected that the girl had been summoned to return by her parents lest she lose her opportunity to vie for the exalted station of Duchess-of-Grade-to-be.

204

She promised to oblige her ladyship, and they stood and talked until the first dance had been brought to an end. Then, together, they went in search of Brent and found him, engaged in cheery conversation with his first partner, Lady Philomena.

"My Lord, I beg your pardon, but I do not think you have met Lady Clarinda—"

Brent snapped: "Where the devil did you run off to? Phoebe, I must talk—"

"My lord, I present Lady Clarinda!" she retorted and turned at once to Lady Philomena, quickly engaging her in conversation.

Brent gave her a look of annoyance and turned to Lady Clarinda, easily all charm and good humor.

It happened again. Phoebe could not get away. Another lady, believing that his lordship had not taken sufficient notice of her, requested Phoebe to remedy the lack—not in so many words, but that was Phoebe's impression of what lay behind the lady's otherwise unwarranted bonhomie.

She hesitated, for she did not think it a kindness to Brent to intrude upon him again and looked to see where he was at. It came as something of a shock to discover that he was no longer with Lady Clarinda, but that Lady Philomena was back in conversation with him. She forgot all about intruding upon Brent and literally dragged over this latest admirer of his and, without a by-your-leave, deposited the girl before Brent and went off again.

That was truly the beginning of an arduous evening for her. Never again was Brent enabled to spend more than a few minutes with any female, except he was out on the floor dancing with her. As soon as the music ended, Phoebe was right there to introduce him to someone new. What Brent thought of her helpfulness can easily be imagined, and he would have liked to have taken Phoebe aside and remonstrated with her—at least, but the demands of being the gentleman of the hour precluded that, and he had to swallow his pique and put a good face on it.

His Grace, engaged with a number of his cronies on the other side of the room, took note of his young relatives and their activities and was in very good humor for the rest of the evening. His friends began to suspect that he was slightly in his cups, for he kept chuckling to himself most of the time.

At breakfast the next morning, Phoebe was surprised to find that her uncle had preceded her to the table and was waiting for her. Usually, she was the first to come down in the morning, it being necessary for her to consult with the help concerning the routines and special tasks to be accomplished for the day.

"Good morning, Uncle Janus. I pray you spent a restful night."

"Good morning, my dear. Yes, I had a most enjoyable evening and slept like a babe. I wished you had not gone off so, after I made the announcement. I had a need to confer with you about it."

"With me, your Grace? To what end, may I ask? Surely no comment of mine could have affected your decision once it had been made and executed."

"Hmmmmm. I see *you* did not spend so comfortable a night. I do declare you are as grouchy as a bear this morning. It promises to be a most excellent day, too."

"Far be it from me, your Grace, to put a damper on

it, but someone else has. It is raining without and bids fair to be a miserable day."

"All the more reason that there should be joy and sunshine within, my child."

Phoebe glanced at him sharply. "Uncle, are you sure you are feeling quite well?"

"Never better, my dear. Never better—now, where in thunderation is that cousin of yours? If I, at my age, can be at table for breakfast at a reasonable time, I should think that he, at his age, should have no trouble at all."

"It could be, your Grace, that my Lord Marquis had overexerted himself to a degree. I swear there were times when I think his lordship was managing to dance with more than one lady at a time! It is no wonder the dear boy has not put in an appearance as yet."

Exclaimed Brent, coming into the room: "It is a positive wonder that the dear boy is able to make any appearance at all this morning, thanks to the thoughtfulness of his cousin who could not stand to see him standing alone with only one or two ladies at a time. Dammit all, Phoebe, I'll thank you to let me do my own dallying! In my own way and in my own time!"

"I only wished to make sure you did not overlook any likely prospect—"

"Prospect be damned! Some of those females you managed to foist off upon me were the most prospectless females one could possibly imagine!"

Phoebe calmly asked: "My Lord Marquis, are you going to stand about all day, gibbering, or will you condescend to take breakfast with us?"

"For heaven's sake, girl, do you have to make such a thing of it? It is only a courtesy title, you know."

"Enough, I say!" snapped the duke impatiently.

"Let us get down to business and leave the bickering for your leisure. I am anxious to know if my acknowledgement of you helped in any way?"

"Oh, I am sure it did, Uncle Janus!" declared Phoebe. "Just look at his lordship! He is grinning fit to be tied. I daresay he has made up his mind, and we can begin to look forward to a new Duchess of Grade."

"Will you cease your chattering, Phoebe!" cried the duke, irately. "For heaven's sake, girl, what a comment to make in my presence, especially while I am trying to eat my egg and toast! Let me assure you it will be longish time before whoever Brent weds is exalted to duchess. I have every intention of staying on for a bit, much to your and his disappointment!"

"Oh, I beg your pardon, Uncle Janus!" exclaimed Phoebe, flushing with embarrassment. "I never meant it that way, I assure you, your Grace."

"And still we chatter! Brent, disregard her and tell me whom you have your eye on."

"Gladly, Uncle. You know, seeing all those charming young ladies—all of them gathered to do me honor —fair made my head swim—"

"More like it drowned in its own vanity—"

"Phoebe!" shouted his Grace.

Phoebe bit her lip and sank deep into her chair.

"My lord, you got as far as your head drowning— er—I mean swimming—Blast you, Phoebe!"

He turned to Brent. "Proceed, if you please!"

Brent shrugged. "Well now, I am not about to say that I am particularly pining for any one of them—on the other hand, a number of the young ladies could easily qualify as your new grandniece."

"Yes, yes, I am sure I am not so particular. Get on with it, man!"

"Er—we might begin with Lady Philomena, a lovely creature and quite charming, too. A man could do worse—"

"But he could do better, I am sure!" interjected Phoebe. "She is exceptionally high-nosed, that one, and could never get along with Uncle Janus. Now, why don't you take Lady Jane. She may not be so beautiful, but she has character and would make a most unexceptional wife."

"Cousin, as it is I who has to do the marrying, I pray you will leave the choosing to me!" retorted Brent. "Who is Lady Jane?"

"The Crossley girl, I am sure you remember her. She was dressed in white gauze striped with blue—"

"Oh, that one! No, I thank you, Cousin. I know you will think it odd in me, but if I had to choose between Lady Jane and Lady Philomena, it must be the latter."

"Well, that is nothing to me, I am sure. She will be your wife, and it will be you who suffers for it," replied Phoebe with a toss of her head.

"Ah, I am so glad you understand. For a moment I feared that I must be beholden to you for my choice of wife," he responded with great irony in his tone.

"Marry her! I could not care less!"

"Then, by your leave, I shall proceed to the next prospect. Sir, now there is Lady Clarinda. There is something of the wench about her, and I will admit that is not a quality to be disdained in a wife, necessarily—"

"Hussy!" muttered Phoebe under her breath.

"—I should like to do a little more thinking in that quarter," continued Brent without pausing.

The duke raised his hand. "A moment, my lord. Phoebe, you had a comment?"

"No, your Grace. It was nothing."

"Now, do you let me be the judge of that. If you have something to say, I should be pleased to hear it. After all, this is a most serious business, and, by rights, the entire family ought to be here assembled to assist Brent in this decision which must bear so heavily upon the fate of the Harewoods. A future Duchess of Grade must be naught if not impeccable in character and breeding. As for her appearance, that I am willing to leave to Brent to judge. He will have to live with her."

"But don't you see, Uncle Janus, my cousin is so taken up with the looks of the different parties that he has no thought for their more important qualities."

"My dear," replied the duke, "I am not seeking a wife; therefore, I suggest you make your remarks to your cousin. I am sure he will appreciate their disinterested wisdom."

"Really, your Grace," Brent protested, "I do not see the need of my cousin's presence at this discussion. It is a highly personal matter and cannot possibly concern her."

His Grace looked to Phoebe for a response. She obliged him.

"I quite agree with you, Cousin, that it is a highly personal matter, the selecting of the wife of the future head of the Harewoods, and that is precisely why I am concerned as must be every other member of our family. Nor do I see any reason for you to be embarrassed by my presence as we are certainly not discussing matters of the heart."

"Whether we are or not, the question of my future wife is my concern and mine alone, I'll have you know!" retorted Brent sharply.

His Grace nodded encouragingly and turned his attention to Phoebe who immediately shot back: "Then how, may I ask, does it concern his Grace if it is all that intimate?"

His Grace's head turned quickly to Brent as though he had no wish to miss the slightest nuance in the exchange.

Brent said, and with great distaste: "His Grace has *made* it his business!"

His Grace turned his head so sharply back to Phoebe that it almost snapped his neck, and he brought his hand up to ease his collar.

Phoebe's eyes glittered, half-closed, as she pronounced with deadly tones: "And I have made it *mine*!"

Brent cast a look of appeal to the duke who was nodding as he sat back in his chair.

"Uncle, I pray you will excuse my cousin. Surely you cannot agree with her?" he asked, uncertainly.

"Now, Nephew, I think she has made a most excellent point. As I see the matter, it is exactly as she has said: we are speaking of the next Duchess of Grade who, only of necessity, must be your wife—certainly that latter is of concern only to yourself; whereas the former is of concren to all of us in this room and the world as well. If I did not feel compelled to see the business done and done quickly before you run through the family fortune, I should have summoned all of the Harewoods to this discussion. They have every right to be included. If that is what you would prefer, I will take it under consideration—but I warn you, I am inclined to favor just having Phoebe by. She has got more sense than the rest of the family put together, excluding myself, of course—but not you, of course, if you understand me."

"All I understand, Uncle, is that you refuse to treat me as a grown man who is up to the mark."

"Ah, my estimate of your understanding increases by leaps and bounds," retorted his Grace with an impertinent grin.

Brent chuckled. "Very well, Phoebe stays—but I still do not see the point of all this. I am not about to make up my mind upon such a serious matter with my brain all cloudy from a night of festivity."

Snapped Phoebe: "Considering how well you do with a clear mind, Cousin, it may well be an improvement!"

The duke's grin turned to a smile of satisfaction as he gave ear to Brent's response. But he was disappointed in that Brent ignored his cousin's remark.

"Your Grace, it boils down to this: I daresay that amongst the ladies I met with and conversed with last night, there are a number whose prospects, from my point of view, are quite reasonable—"

"Precisely who are they?" demanded Phoebe. "You have yet to say!"

Staring grimly into her eyes, Brent spread his fingers and began to count upon them: "First there is Lady Philomena—"

"But she is never—"

"Cousin, you demanded to know my thinking, and I am telling it to you! Now, shut your mouth and hearken to me!—First, there is the Lady Philomena—"

"Uncle Janus," cried Phoebe, "you cannot let him marry Philomena Cogswell!"

"Blast you, Phoebe!" exploded Brent, "I never said that I was going to marry her! I am merely listing, for your diversion, the ladies that I shall consider—when I come to consider them!"

Phoebe's lips were atremble. "V-very w-well, wh-who else is there?"

His Grace's eyes were half-lidded, and there was a wry smile upon his lips.

Brent, his forefinger upon the forefinger of his other hand, went on: "I think we can eliminate the Doddington female—"

Phoebe swallowed hard. "At least, w-we agree on that. And—?"

"Lady Martha is not to be discounted, although, in my opinion, she does not hold a candle to Lady Philomena."

Said his Grace: "I do not see the necessity for protracting this discussion. It appears to me that Lady Philomena has made some sort of an impression upon you, and, as far as I am concerned, I will approve and gladly. The marriage settlement in that quarter will be quite handsome. Your future station will make the bargain with the Cogswells."

"I say, your Grace, do not rush me! I still would like to mull things over a bit, don't you know!" protested Brent.

"Nonsense!" retorted his Grace. "Between now and a fortnight hence, I venture to say that your mind will not change—"

"Yet do I request the time! It is not an easy—"

"Brent, I tell you it will change nothing. Let us suppose that the time for your decision had been now—this very instant—you would choose Lady Philomena. Am I not right?"

Brent stared at him. "It is not fair to put the question to me like that!"

"What has fairness got to say to it? We are not talking of sport! This is no game, young man! You are about to make the one most important decision of

213

your life, one that *I* could never come to—and I do sympathize with you. But it is necessary that I put *my* affairs in order and the succession *is* my affair. Unfortunately for you, as you are the successor in question, you have got to make up your mind, and fairness has not a thing to do with it! Now, it will be Philomena, will it not? I might as well begin to talk with Lord Cogswell and get the business started. After all, you are not my favorite, and I am quite anxious to get the Cogswells—or whoever—to share the burden of your upkeep with me as soon as possible."

"Such a depth of affection that an uncle could have for a nephew is remarkable," replied Brent.

"Yes, well, I await your word on it."

Brent stared hard at him. Then he turned to look at Phoebe. She sat staring stonily at him, all dead within.

It is perhaps the full length of a minute that Brent continued to regard her. Finally he sighed and nodded. "Aye, the Lady Philomena, your Grace."

It proved too much for Phoebe. Her composure, that she had been to the end of her resources to maintain, came all to pieces and she fell to weeping silently. She sat, still staring in Brent's direction, but she saw nothing, so bedewed were her eyes, and the tears overflowed and spilled down her cheeks.

"Blast your liver, Uncle!" shouted Brent, rising abruptly to his feet. "And blast all settlements! I shall marry whom I damn well please!"

"An' she pleases me, I shall confer my blessings upon the pair of you," responded the duke quite calmly. "I am quite easily satisfied, you know. If she be finely bred and exceptionally well-endowed, financially that is, I ask nothing more of her."

Brent went to stand behind Phoebe and, tenderly

placing his hands upon her shoulders, declared: "Phoebe shall be my bride, and I shall countenance no objections from anyone, be he duke or king!"

"Hmmm—those are awfully strong sentiments. And what, may I ask, will you say to it if Phoebe objects?"

"I—I—" Brent looked startled and bent at once to her. She lifted her hand, placed it upon his on her shoulder, and raised a glowing, if damp, face to his.

Completely disregarding his Grace, a very interested observer, Brent lifted Phoebe from out of her chair and pressed her to him, planting a kiss upon her lips that was at once a declaration and an apology. Phoebe's response indicated unmistakably an acceptance of both.

"Ahem!" said his Grace after a reasonable lapse of time, and the lovers broke apart.

Brent, his arm wrapped about Phoebe's waist in a most possessive manner, glared defiance at his Grace. "Sir, do you have any objections?"

"You have already declared that nothing I can say will dissuade you. I shall not waste my breath."

"But, Uncle," pleaded Phoebe, "your blessing must be a most important consideration to us both. Brent is upset, and you must not mind too much what he says."

"So you would have my approval, young lady? Is that it, or is it my pocketbook that is of the first consideration."

"Your Grace, if you were indigent, still should I hope for your approval and blessing; but, as you are rich beyond counting, I should be a hypocrite to say that that does not concern me. I have a wish to be proud of my husband, and poverty leaves something to be desired in that quarter, don't you agree? In my case, I should be happy if we had your blessing unadorned by anything of your pocketbook."

"Brent, does your bride-to-be speak for you as well?" asked his Grace.

"Aye, you are a crab at times, but one can get used to that, for you are fair-minded, in something of an unscrupulous manner—"

The duke broke into chuckles and exclaimed: "Aye, Nephew, I bear some affection for you, too! Well, then, I must disappoint you for I shall never approve this union."

"Oh, Uncle Janus!" exclaimed Phoebe, tears welling up to her eyes.

"So be it!" said Brent heavily. "We shall just have to make our own way—but I tell you, I do not think it at all fair that you hold Phoebe's poverty against her. It cannot be her breeding! Hers is as fine as your own!"

"Well, it is certainly not her lack of wealth, my fine fellow! As she stands there in your arm, she is wealthy enough for my taste. It gives me the greatest pleasure, Nephew, to point out to you, sir, that, here in this room, I have but one poor relation, and that is you, sir—for as long as I live that is."

"Uncle Janus, whatever do you mean?" asked Phoebe, extremely puzzled.

"Simply this, young lady: When Travers, my man of business, came to call that day, it was for more than putting yon scapegrace in his place. I executed a settlement upon you that makes you wealthy enough to pick where you choose. I should be damned beyond redemption if I were to tolerate my niece and my housekeeper to continue on in such a disgraceful state of penury. Your Aunt Sophia's portion, which came to me upon her demise, I have passed on to you, with all the rest of her duties and privileges."

"By God, you are a villain, sir!" exclaimed Brent. "Now it must seem to all the world that I am marrying Phoebe for her money!"

His Grace chuckled maliciously. "I doubt it very much that your *love* gives a damn for what the world thinks."

"Phoebe!" cried Brent. "This makes all the difference—"

Phoebe, her hands upon her hips, wheeled upon him and, shaking a finger up into his face, exclaimed: "You, sir, are a nodcock—"

"My sentiments, precisely," agreed the duke.

"—if you are going to stand there and tell me that it is all very well for you to marry Philomena Cogswell for her money, but that it is not at all the thing to marry me for the same reason. I am as good as she!"

"Oh, I say! That is not it at all! I'd marry you even if you had not a copper—"

"Oh ho! So you did have it in mind to marry that witch!" cried Phoebe.

"Heaven forfend! Phoebe, you know I had never the intention! I was merely playing for time—"

"Well, then what is your excuse now, when there is not the slightest need? His Grace has said quite plainly that I may marry whom I list, and I would marry you!"

Brent stood there for a moment, completely baffled. He raised a hand and scratched his head. Turning to the duke, he asked: "Damme, sir, how did I get into this?"

"I know this young lady of old, my boy, and if you will heed my advice, I suggest you get out of the

217

business as gracefully as you can—if you have the wit!"

Brent stared at the duke uncomprehendingly, and the duke stared back at him, very slowly and deliberately winking his eye. Without a further word, Brent turned and caught Phoebe abruptly to him. Staring down into her face, he said: "Very well, Cousin, I am completely shameless. I shall marry you for your money."

And he soundly kissed her. Phoebe was gurgling happily when they both of them finally terminated the caress and turned to the patient duke.

"Then you do give us your blessing, Uncle Janus?" she asked.

"Absolutely not! You marry against my wishes—"

"But why do you persist in objecting—"

"How would you like it if your housekeeper ran off and got married, leaving you, old and helpless, to fend for yourself?" demanded the duke.

Phoebe and Brent exchanged glances. He nodded.

Phoebe turned to the duke and said: "Uncle Janus, I am sure we shall be happy to come to you for a visit every now and again."

"I want you here at Pickering Hall! The place will not be the same without you!" he retorted stubbornly.

"Well, I suppose—for a time—but you will not mind if we go on a honeymoon, surely. The place will not come tumbling down for a little while yet."

"Ah, that is better, and I have picked out just the spot for your honeymoon, too."

"You have?" exclaimed Phoebe and Brent in a chorus of disappointment.

"Aye. Grade!"

"Grade!"

"Grade. Have you ever been to Grade?"

218

They both of them shook their heads.

"It is on the Cornish coast. There are cliffs and beaches and the surf roaring and"—he paused for effect—"there is solitude—as much as a pair of young lovers could wish. And just to give you something to occupy your time, Brent and yourself can look in on the place and see to it how whatever needs improving can be, so that it all will not be a sheer waste of time. You cannot object, I am sure, since it must be Brent's business to see to the fortunes which he is to inherit, especially as there is bound to be something of an increase in the Maitland-Harewood branch, wouldn't you say—sooner or later, that is."

"And after?" asked Phoebe, while Brent's face clouded over.

"Why, after your honeymoon, I shall expect you back here with me at the Hall. There is plenty of room."

Brent would have objected, but Phoebe squeezed his hand and spoke instead: "Very well, your Grace, it shall be as you say. There are not many children who can boast of having been reared by a duke from birth—"

"Here now, Phoebe! The devil you say!" exclaimed his Grace, for once discomposed. "I have no wish to have your brats foisted off upon me!"

"Well, since you insist we stay with you, when they arrive, they shall have to be all about, don't you know. Or do you have some idea of parceling them out to a foundling's home?"

The duke fell back in his chair. "That is not so bad an idea as you may think!" he growled, insincerely, as he stared about him. "Well then, dammit, you shall have to come here to live, for I surely am not up to running the place—and I shall take an apartment in

London whenever your brood begins to make its appearance. There! That should settle it. The wedding will be next month, and I expect you will see to it that it is a bang-up affair!"

"Me? But I am the bride-to-be!" protested Phoebe.

"And you are also the Mistress of Pickering Hall and like to be forever. I'll not trust the preparations to anyone else!"

Phoebe stared at her uncle, and there was a strained look in her face. Finally she said: "Uncle Janus, I am beginning to suspect a plot. I do declare that you had it in mind all this time that Brent and I should wed."

"Well, of course I did! You can hardly have believed I was ever about to let that imbecile wed outside of the family, did you—and anyway, once I was assured how it was with you, I was obliged to see you get your wish. One must keep one's housekeeper content, you know. Believe me, the good ones don't grow on trees."

He arose from the table and bowed to them. "My lord, my lady, may you keep your rejoicing down to a mild roar. I am going to the reading room for a bit—although I am sure I shall not hear a peep out of you."

Grinning with self-satisfaction, he picked up his stick; then, casting it aside, he strolled out of the room.

Phoebe turned to Brent, only to discover that her love was fuming.

"Why, that crotchety old blackguard! He has been toying with us these many days!"

Phoebe raised a hand to his lips. "My love, do not hold it against him. He was only trying to insure our happiness, I am sure—and his comfort, of course; but

220

think! We shall have all of Pickering Hall to ourselves for a while."

Brent smiled and kissed her hand. "Aye, that is a thought to hang one's hat on! Pickering Hall without Uncle Janus could be heaven, I am thinking."

Beyond that point, their discussion was no less eloquent for lack of any worthwhile oral expression.

His Grace, the Duke of Grade, walked into the reading room, the smug smile still wreathing his lips.

"Ah, that was a good day's work, and it is not eleven o'clock yet."

He picked up the day's paper and sat down in his armchair. Shaking it out, he began his daily perusal only to stop and let it drop into his lap as he gazed off into space.

"I am sure I shall not like it in the city. I am too old for that sort of life. Split me if I should be dull enough to let them put me out of my house and home! By damn they shall not! I daresay I can be as good a grandfather to their brats as the next one! Devil take it, I shall stay! Oh, good Lord! It is a great-grandfather I shall have to be!" He paused to ruminate over that disconcerting thought.

Finally a smile broke forth on his lips. "Now, that is not so bad! No one can expect all that much effort from a great-grandfather, now can they? Oh, won't they be overjoyed to hear it!" And he chuckled so hard, he wound up in a fit of coughing.

ALL TIME BESTSELLERS
FROM POPULAR LIBRARY

Reading Fit For A Queen

QUEEN-SIZE GOTHICS are a new idea. They offer the very best in novels of romantic suspense, by the top writers, greater in length and drama, richer in reading pleasure.

☐ THE FOUR MARYS—Rinalda Roberts	00366-9	1.25
☐ GRAVE'S COMPANY—S. Nichols	00252-2	1.25
☐ GRENENCOURT—I. Charles	00264-6	1.25
☐ THE HARLAN LEGACY— Jo Anne Creighton	03206-5	1.50
☐ THE HEMLOCK TREE—E. Lottman	00235-2	1.25
☐ INN OF EVIL—J.A. Creighton	00224-7	1.25
☐ ISLAND OF SILENCE— Carolyn Brimley Norris	00411-8	1.25
☐ ISLAND OF THE SEVEN HILLS—Z. Cass	00277-8	1.25
☐ KEYS OF HELL—L. Osborne	00284-0	1.25
☐ THE KEYS TO QUEENSCOURT— Jeanne Hines (Empress)	08508-8	1.75
☐ THE LAZARUS INHERITANCE (Large type)—Noel Vreeland Carter	00432-0	1.25
☐ THE LEGEND OF WITCHWYND (Large Type)—Jeanne Hines	00420-7	1.25
☐ LET THE CRAGS COMB OUT HER DAINTY HAIR—J. Marten	00302-2	1.25
☐ LUCIFER WAS TALL—Elizabeth Gresham	00346-4	1.25
☐ MIDNIGHT SAILING—S. Hufford	00263-8	1.25
☐ THE MIRACLE AT ST. BRUNO'S— Philippa Carr (Empress)	08533-9	1.75
☐ OF LOVE INCARNATE—Jane Crowcroft	00418-5	1.25

Buy them at your local bookstores or use this handy coupon for ordering:

Popular Library, P.O. Box 5755, Terre Haute, Indiana 47805   B-10

Please send me the books I have checked above. Orders for less than 5 books must include 60c for the first book and 25c for each additional book to cover mailing and handling. Orders of 5 or more books postage is Free. I enclose $_____in check or money order.

Name_____

Address_____

City_____ State/Zip_____

Please allow 4 to 5 weeks for delivery. This offer expires 6/78.